✓ 2m 5/88
2m5/97
W9-ARO-325

Her face glowed in the firelight

"Have you been bored living back here?" Steve asked, breaking the silence of the night.

Susan turned to face him. "Not bored. Lonely, maybe." Her gaze didn't waver from his.

"I've been lonely, too, Susan. Far too lonely."

She took a deep bolstering breath. "Hold me?"

He took her gladly into his arms. His hand stroked her hair again and again, each motion more soothing than the last.

Need welled up within her, dark and fierce. No one else had ever made her feel this way, safe and loved, with just a touch, a look or a quiet word. She inhaled and was suddenly aware of a love so strong and deep it hurt. Tears misted her eyes, sorrow flooded her—regret for all they had lost. Then, like a bursting dam, the emotion she'd been holding back for so long poured out in a silent stream of tears.

"Keep on holding me," she whispered.

ABOUT THE AUTHOR

Cathy Gillen Thacker is a full-time novelist who once taught piano to children. Born and raised in Ohio, she attended Miami University, and after moving cross-country several times, she now resides in Texas with her husband and three children.

Books by Cathy Gillen Thacker

HARLEQUIN AMERICAN ROMANCE
37—TOUCH OF FIRE
75—PROMISE ME TODAY
102—HEART'S JOURNEY
134—REACH FOR THE STARS

HARLEQUIN TEMPTATION
47—EMBRACE ME, LOVE
82—A PRIVATE PASSION

These books may be available at your local bookseller.

Don't miss any of our special offers. Write to us at the following address for information on our newest releases.

Harlequin Reader Service
P.O. Box 52040, Phoenix, AZ 85072-2040
Canadian address: P.O. Box 2800, Postal Station A,
5170 Yonge St., Willowdale, Ont. M2N 6J3

Reach for the Stars

CATHY GILLEN THACKER

Harlequin Books

TORONTO • NEW YORK • LONDON
AMSTERDAM • PARIS • SYDNEY • HAMBURG
STOCKHOLM • ATHENS • TOKYO • MILAN

To Charlie, Julie, David and Sarah—with love.

Published January 1986

First printing November 1985

ISBN 0-373-16134-4

Copyright © 1986 by Cathy Gillen Thacker. All rights reserved.
Philippine copyright 1986. Australian copyright 1986.
Except for use in any review, the reproduction or utilization of
this work in whole or in part in any form by any electronic,
mechanical or other means, now known or hereafter invented,
including xerography, photocopying and recording, or in any
information storage or retrieval system, is forbidden without
the permission of the publisher, Harlequin Enterprises Limited,
225 Duncan Mill Road, Don Mills, Ontario, Canada M3B 3K9.

All the characters in this book have no existence outside the
imagination of the author and have no relation whatsoever to
anyone bearing the same name or names. They are not even
distantly inspired by any individual known or unknown to the
author, and all the incidents are pure invention.

The Harlequin trademarks, consisting of the words
HARLEQUIN AMERICAN ROMANCE, HARLEQUIN
AMERICAN ROMANCES, and the portrayal of a Harlequin,
are trademarks of Harlequin Enterprises Limited; the portrayal
of a Harlequin is registered in the United States Patent and
Trademark Office and in the Canada Trade Marks Office.

Printed in Canada

Chapter One

"Steve called. He wants to see you."

Susan set her suitcase down in the middle of her bedroom floor and faced her mother, exasperated. There was no denying it; hope for a reconciliation sprang eternal in that woman's heart. Susan walked to the window and glanced through white lace curtains at the quiet residential street below. After living in Michigan for a year, she needed time to reacquaint herself with her roots. She needed to plan for her future. "Steve said everything there was to say when we ended our engagement nine months ago."

"He was hurting. You both were."

"And even more after he told me what he thought of my supposedly 'limitless' ambition. There's no way I'm putting myself through that torture again." Susan paused, her suspicions hardening her tone. "How did he know I was back in West Virginia?"

Her mother shrugged, looking undeniably guilty as she arranged a vase of fresh flowers on the vanity beside Susan's pink-and-white calico-covered bed. Since Susan had gone away to college, she had used the bedroom only sporadically, on visits. It was still decorated in teenage style, complete with brightly colored posters, stuffed animals and assorted memorabilia from her high school and college days. These days Susan felt as if she were entering a time warp every time she walked through the door.

"Mom, did *you* tell him I was coming back to West Virginia to live?" Susan demanded. Though her mother believed otherwise, Susan considered the move only a temporary one and had put all her furniture into storage.

"Not Steve, precisely, no." Emma Trent smoothed her oversized blue-and-white pin-striped shirt over slender hips. In sneakers and jeans, the fifty-five-year-old woman sported boundless energy, sparkling blue-green eyes and short-cropped hair that was still more chestnut brown than gray.

"But you did tell others." Susan didn't know whether to cry or appreciate her mother's gesture.

"Of course I did! Your father and I both did! You know how long we've looked forward to having you near us again. For heaven's sake, Susan, how long do you think you can live here before everyone in Grafton realizes you're back?" With a Taylor County grapevine more efficient than Ma Bell's long-distance lines and a father situated as superintendent of district schools, Susan knew it wouldn't be long now.

She sighed and sat down on her bed, crossing her long legs at the knee. She knew her mother meant well, and that made it hard for her to stay angry. "I didn't want to have to confront Steve my first day back." Susan raked a hand through her dark hair. At least with her mother she didn't have to pretend.

Emma sat down beside Susan, capturing her hand. "I'm sorry about that. But maybe it's for the best; maybe it's time you did see Steve."

Susan pulled away and paced to the window again. "Ever his champion, aren't you?"

Emma followed her daughter to the window. "Steve is a very dear and wonderful man. I've always thought that. The fact you're no longer engaged doesn't change that."

As far as Steve's qualities were concerned, Emma was correct. Steve was part saint, part jester, part Valentino. He had always possessed the ability to make her laugh, to make her feel, to make her cry. He inspired a range of emotion in her that no one else ever had.

Her mother's expression softened. "I'm sorry, sweetheart. I know this is painful for you, that the past few months have been anything but easy and that you've been under a lot of stress, both on and off the job."

"You can say that again." Susan forced a wry smile. She wondered just how much Steve knew of what she had been through.

"I'll stop meddling," Susan's mother promised abruptly, striding toward the door. She turned, hesitant again as she added, "But I can't change our plans for this evening."

Susan felt herself cringe slightly. She'd kept the time of her homecoming purposely vague, stating only that she'd arrive either Wednesday or early Thursday. She planned to circumvent any elaborate welcome homes; but apparently her mother had bargained on the sooner time—and won. "What do you mean 'plans'?" Susan asked anxiously.

"Steve's reelection committee is meeting here tonight."

Susan glanced at her watch coolly, ignoring the sudden racing of her pulse. "When is everyone due?"

"In less than an hour, which means dinner will be a fix-it-yourself affair. There's plenty of food in the fridge." She paused. "You could help us, Susan."

In answer, Susan gave a short, disbelieving sigh.

Her mother's brows arched. "You helped him get elected before," she reminded.

"That was before we...broke up."

Emma said nothing. Susan knew her mother thought she had been a fool to ever leave West Virginia to pursue a "glamorous" career. And in a sense Emma had been right. Part of her journey had brought nothing but heartache. "He's still the same man he was," her mother reminded gently.

"And still very difficult for me to be around." Needing to be busy, Susan reached decisively for the clothes on hangers and opened her closet door. She took a step back, viewing the contents. Gone was much of the clutter she'd left. Front and center was white satin and yards of seed pearls. It was her wedding dress, which had once seemed to her the most beautiful garment ever made. But by quirk of fate and broken hearts, the day to wear it had never materialized.

"Oh, Susan." Emma's regret was evident in her voice, "I meant to put that in my closet before you got here." She had discretely removed the gown the last time Susan had been home, and the time before that.

Her mother rushed on, explaining, "I just—I hate to put something that valuable and lovely in the basement, damp as it sometimes gets." Susan wrung her hands together.

As it had already been altered to fit Susan's tall, slim form, it was impossible to return the gown. "It's all right, Mom." Susan smiled calmly. "You were right to save it. Maybe we'll even find someone to give it to." With effort, she pushed the dress aside slightly, careful not to wrinkle it. As she hung up her street clothes, she felt a turmoil of emotion that led her closer to tears than she wanted to admit.

"Look, there's no reason to leave it there; I'll just put it in my closet." Susan's mother stepped forward.

Susan put out a hand to discourage Emma. "Mom, stop. Ignoring my broken engagement won't change anything. We can't go on hiding the dress forever."

Suddenly, her old bedroom seemed claustrophobic. "I've changed my mind. I'll unpack later. Right now I just need to relax."

Susan's mother followed her out the bedroom door. Together they descended the sweeping oak steps to the first floor of the turn-of-the-century house. "I think I'll go out for a walk," Susan said impulsively when they'd reached the front hall. Walking was her method of working off excess tension, and fortunately it nearly always worked. Reading the concern on her mother's face, she said, "I'm fine, Mom, really I am. But it's been a long day, and I need some time alone."

"You're not going to change first?" Her mother looked critically at Susan's city clothes. Feeling it important that she return from her stint in Lansing as polished and elegantly dressed as when she had left to take the job, Susan had worn a tailored skirt and matching cardigan jacket in deep periwinkle blue for the drive home. The white silk shirt she wore beneath was cut in a sophisticated V. Though slightly impractical for such a long trip, the clothing had made her feel better about leaving Lansing and returning home. She'd been able to perceive going back to West Virginia as another step in the journey forward. However, neither her bone-colored pumps nor the slim skirt were made for walking. But to change clothes would mean unpacking further, and she certainly wasn't in the mood for that.

Susan reached for her handbag and slung it casually over her shoulder. "I won't be going far. I'll be fine." Working to erase the mental image of the wedding dress, she added, "Maybe I'll stop in at the corner drugstore and buy some odds and ends, or even take in a movie downtown."

Her mother said nothing until Susan had reached the front porch. "What about Steve? Won't you at least call him back? He sounded very determined on the phone. You're not going to be able to avoid him forever," Emma warned.

"Maybe not, Mom, but I meant what I said about needing time." Susan left. As she anticipated, the walk in the fresh air was calming. The peaceful aura of the city surrounded her like a welcoming cloak. How easy it would be to fall back into the unhurried pace, Susan mused. She could at least relieve herself temporarily from the fierce work pressure she had been under.

She passed several crosswalks, waited dutifully at the first two posts for the walk sign to appear, but impatiently started crossing at the third. The October air was crisp and cool, devoid of city pollution and gasoline exhaust. Susan felt familiar with the residential streets lined with rambling white frame houses. Most were at least half a century old, but all were in excellent shape. The wide front porches were decorated with chain-hung swings, potted plants and a scattered array of toys and children.

A wealth of hickory and magnolia, ash and oak trees shaded the streets and sidewalks. Fallen buckeyes, walnuts and pecans littered the ground. The leaves were changing color, reflecting a bonanza of shimmering russet and gold, orange and bronze.

Grafton's claim to fame was the origination of Mother's Day—the holiday had started in 1908 when town resident Anna Jarvis observed the anniversary of her mother's death. In Susan's mind not much else of staggering importance had happened since. Oh, there were the requisite number of service industries needed to support a city population of close to seven thousand people. And there were certainly enough fast-food restaurants and grocery, drug, department and hardware stores in existence to provide the essentials. There were even two hotels, the largest with forty rooms. And a recently built Lean Delight food factory contributed to the local economy by supplying some three hundred and fifty jobs for area women. Other local residents made their living raising livestock or working in the Taylor County Coal Mine.

Grafton was a quiet place with good schools and people who cared. It would make a good place to retire someday, Susan mused. But for now she wanted much more career excitement and opportunity than the sleepy Blue Ridge town could offer.

Abruptly, Susan became aware of a car following her at the curb. Not wanting to appear alarmed, she turned only slightly, noticing a tan-and-brown sedan with a sheriff's emblem emblazoned on the door. Susan stifled a groan of dismay. Inside the car was Sheriff Steve Markham. He held a radio speaker to his mouth. Because his windows were rolled up, she couldn't make out what he was saying. But she knew she didn't want to talk to him, not yet, maybe not ever.

Her next decision was easy. She swiftly did an about-face, so sleek and sharp it would have been the envy of her high-school marching-band days, and slicing behind the patrol car, cut swiftly across the street, narrowly missing a car coming from the opposite direction.

Two seconds later the patrol car was turning around in the closet driveway. Susan gritted her teeth as she heard the patrol car thrust into reverse, back up, then switch into forward gear. She grimaced even more when, red light flashing, the sedan pulled up smoothly in front of her, without even the slightest screeching of tires. She supposed she should be glad Steve hadn't turned on his siren, alerting everyone in the neighborhood to her return.

Steve had come to West Virginia four years earlier on vacation. He'd immediately fallen in love with the rugged terrain and the wild mountains and decided he and West Virginia were meant for one another. Learning there were jobs available in area law enforcement, the veteran New York City cop shortly secured a job as a deputy. A month later, he and his teenage brother were residents of the Grafton community. Susan had been living in Cincinnati by that time, working as a consumer-advocate reporter. They met on one of her subsequent visits home, when both had attended a party given by Patsy and Frank Winter. The attraction between them had been instantaneous, and very potent. Over the course of the next two and a half years they'd seen one another steadily despite the fact they lived nearly 250 miles apart.

The slamming of a car door jerked her from her reverie. "Hello, Susan." Steve's voice was even as he stepped around the front of the car.

"Steve." Her greeting was crisp, detached. She paused, turning to confront him as he neared. With something akin to disappointment, she noted there was no smile on his face as he silently regarded her fair skin and wide, thick-lashed turquoise eyes.

Hungry for the sight of him, Susan let her own eyes scan him for a brief moment. Since settling in West Virginia, Steve had adapted well to the unpretentiousness of the rural environment. But traces of his perenially streetwise aura remained. The seemingly inherent sophistication was never more obvious than at that moment, she thought resentfully. The truth was, he didn't look like a small-town sheriff. He never had. His dark ash-blond hair was too unruly, curling impossibly down the back of his neck, just over the tip of his ears. His face was for the most part elegantly oval, yet his jaw remained slightly rough-hewn. His nose was straight and slim, and his eyes were more gray than blue, probing and deeply set beneath thick sun-bleached brows. His naturally tawny skin still bore the traces of his summer tan. He was six feet two to her five ten. Her heels put them closer to equal height.

He gave her a half smile as he withdrew a small notepad from the front pocket of his neatly starched long-sleeved khaki shirt. He began scribbling energetically without looking up. "I'd like to have been able to say it's a pleasure to see you again and leave it at that." His eyes met hers briefly, reminding her of the car she'd just walked in front of in order to avoid him. "I can't. I'm going to have to write you a ticket."

Her mouth formed a silent "oh" in dismay, but she immediately clamped it shut. She wouldn't make a fool of herself by begging him to forget what he was paid to notice. Not that he could have been bribed, anyway. "Fine. Go ahead," she stated nonchalantly, daring him to try and give her a hard time. Holding the office of sheriff gave him power to enforce the laws, but he had no power over her personally. It was time they both accepted that.

His eyes slowly surveyed her heart-shaped face surrounded by a wealth of thick wavy hair. Recently cut to just below her chin, the hairstyle flattered her with sideswept bangs. "Do you have a problem with getting a ticket?" Judging by his grin, he knew she did. "If you have a protest, I'm all ears."

She stiffened her spine slightly, modifying her posture to regal pose. "Just do your job."

After a moment of silence he spoke, and his voice held an exasperated edge. "Fine. Step in the car, please." He motioned toward the sedan.

Her steps sounded staccato on the cement. He opened the door on the passenger side, and she slid in.

Easing behind the wheel, he held open his hand and extended it toward her. "Identification?"

Whatever was left of her self-control suddenly dissipated. "You know damn well who I am," she snapped. Stubbornly, she made no move to open her purse and extract her billfold.

He leaned back, flexing his shoulders against the tan vinyl seat. His chest was wide, simmering with tensile strength. Abruptly, she had the feeling he was as close to losing his temper as she. "Do I? Sometimes I wonder if I ever knew you at all."

"Precisely why I left." Her voice was as icy as she could manage.

Steve sighed heavily, and without preamble, gestured halfway up the block. His voice was curt and authoritative as he explained. "You may or may not have noticed the crosswalks and lights we've recently put at every corner. We've cut down the number of accidents significantly during this past year. In fact, as your own mother, a schoolteacher, can attest to, we've not had one child hit by a car since the calendar year began. Getting adults to follow the traffic pattern has been tougher. So," he continued, giving her a telling look, "we've had to remind them, on paper, so they can be sure to get it right the next time."

She knew how strongly he felt about preventing traffic accidents of any kind. Steve's own parents had been killed in an auto collision, orphaning both him and his brother. The fight went out of her. She had known better than to step out in front of any car. It was lucky she hadn't been hit. And she knew, as did everyone else in Grafton, that Steve was as much concerned with promoting preventive law enforcement as

some doctors were with promoting preventive medi-
cine. "Half a pound of awareness is worth ten times
as much aftermath?" Her light tone was an attempt to
make peace.

He nodded. His smile faded as he said softly, more
reasonably, "You didn't really think I would use the
power of this badge to harass you?"

"No." In her heart, she had known better.

Steve watched her, the steady glance never wavering. In their moment of mutual unguardedness, he was
unendurably accessible. "I wanted to see you," he said
quietly. "Why didn't you return my call?"

"I needed time to sort out my thoughts."

Silence fell between them, like a wellspring of hurts
too deep to ever bridge.

Finally, she found her voice. "I heard you're running for reelection."

Softly, he said, "You're surprised?"

"Yes. I had thought—" She bit her lip, stopping
short. The concerns they'd had previously, when engaged, were no longer valid. Of course he'd want to
stay. He had no reason not to.

"I like living in a small town, Susan." He was
watching her carefully, as if looking for any clue to
what she was thinking.

She smiled, keeping the conversation focused on the
joy of living in a small town. "You like living where
everyone knows one another." Having grown up under that microscope, she now preferred anonymity.

"And cares about one another," he affirmed. In a
less than subtle bid to change the subject, he said,
"I'm sorry about your job."

Her head turned sharply. Humiliation made her shoulders become rigid. "You know my contract wasn't renewed?"

He shrugged, uncomfortably tugging at the tie around his neck. "You're still a celebrity locally, Susan. Everything about you is news, even your unemployment. So yes, news of your release from WJCG in Lansing eventually made the wire services, and then all the papers here."

She felt color blush her cheeks. Having everyone know of her failure only made it that much more debilitating. And to have him know how she must feel— Now her humiliation was complete. "The station was never very successful financially. I knew that going in." She glanced away, resenting his compassion. "I was newest on staff and therefore the first to go when additional budget cuts had to be made."

It had hurt, not having her WJCG contract renewed, especially when she'd worked so hard to achieve her goal. Not that she'd always known she wanted to work in television. After getting a degree in journalism at a state college, she'd been hired as a rookie reporter for a Cincinnati newspaper, doing an occasional consumer-oriented piece along with the usual wedding and birth announcements assigned staff newcomers. Public response to her consumer pieces had been favorable, and she'd soon been given a weekly column in the Sunday paper. That exposure led to occasional guest appearances on a local television station.

During two- to four-minute spots before the camera, Susan explained things like which frozen dinners were of high quality. After prodigious research, she told consumers what to look for when buying a video recorder or signing an apartment lease. To her surprise and delight, Susan thrived on the excitement of live, visual reporting. And her ability to reach large audiences with her consumer news was unsurpassed.

Eventually, because of the viewer interest in the news she covered, the station had decided to make consumer-advocate reports a permanent segment on the late-evening news. Unfortunately for Susan, they awarded the honor of hosting those spots to a full-time staff member-substitute anchor who had earned the airtime over the course of five years. Susan was hurt but understanding. She knew she would have to pay her dues, too, and immediately set out on a path that would enable her to do just that.

With her customary zeal, she had talked to employment counselors who specialized in media work and sent out countless résumés and query letters. Armed with knowledge, she began looking for full-time television work, seeking a job that would also bring her closer geographically to Steve.

Over the next few months, Susan began sending around videotapes of her appearances. For several months, nothing happened. Charleston, Cincinnati, Bluefield and Columbus stations all turned her down. Entry-level positions were nearly impossible to find, and those slots available were being filled by people with more experience. Deeply disappointed but still hopeful, Susan continued her job search in markets that were more distant: Minneapolis, Chicago, Detroit. She invested in recording and making new tapes. Again, nothing. More dejected than ever, she faced the possibility that it might not be possible to work in her chosen medium. She began exploring other possibilities—writing a book, working in radio—anything that might broaden her credentials.

Again, nothing came through. Susan continued working on the Cincinnati newspaper, but her spirits were low. She wanted to be with Steve full-time. She wanted her work. Both she and Steve started looking toward the future. The possibility of marriage had always been there for them, and after two and a half years of steady dating, it seemed like the time to formalize their commitment to one another. And it was at that point, some ten months after Susan's search for a more challenging job had started, that she was offered a contract to write a book.

It seemed like a miracle, or at least an answer to their main problem, if not her long-range career aspiration. Susan accepted the opportunity lightheartedly, not looking much past her immediate future. In short order, she accepted the contract to write a book, quit her job at the paper and moved back to Grafton. She and Steve made wedding preparations.

For two months it seemed Susan's life was perfect. Then, with the wedding just a month away, she received a call from a Michigan television station. The station manager had seen some of her videotapes while visiting a colleague in Cincinnati and heard she was looking for a full-time entry-level job. He had an opening in his Lansing station and he wanted her to take the position immediately. The salary wasn't much more than she'd received at the Cincinnati paper, but it was a start. Susan and Steve discussed the options proposed. Realizing how much she wanted the chance, he encouraged her to take the job. They decided to postpone the wedding, planning at the end of a year's time to reevaluate their situations and decide then what to do. Steve's current term as sheriff would be over in a year, and Susan would have a year of experience under her belt. .

In theory, their plan of action had sounded very modern. But the subsequent reality had proved anything but workable for either of them. In less than three months, their relationship had disintegrated entirely. Both of them were lonely and miserable. Susan resented the fact that Steve hadn't followed her to Lansing. As a cop, she had reasoned, he could get a job practically anywhere. Steve had felt she was putting everything ahead of him, running from commitment by fiercely pursuing a career. In a final effort to resolve their problems, they'd met one last time, in Lansing. The weekend, their first in weeks, had been a disaster from start to finish. Before they'd known it, they'd been fighting. He'd cursed her ambition. She'd sworn at his devotion to West Virginia and the town of Grafton. There'd been an abundance of hurt and too little time to heal it. They ended their engagement by mutual sad agreement. And that was it. Until the present afternoon there had been nine months of silence between them.

Susan didn't know what she had expected to feel upon seeing Steve again. She realized now there was a reason for that. Facing him again, she still felt as hurt, angry, confused and bewildered as she had the day they'd broken up.

The sound of children playing near the street jerked Susan from her reverie. Steve was gazing past the windshield of the patrol car to the canopy of trees beyond. He was as lost in thought as she had been. As if feeling her gaze upon him, he turned back to her. The firm line of his mouth was tightly drawn. After a moment, he spoke quietly. "Why did you come back?"

Susan took a deep breath. *Concentrate on the details,* she thought. *Stick to matters you can discuss.* "Financially, it's important for me to stay in a place with a low cost of living. I also wanted to be near my folks again, at least for a while. After all I've been through, I need their support and their love."

"Then you'll be living with them?" he asked.

"No. I need my own place. I plan to rent the cheapest apartment I can find, though it will have to be furnished. I left the majority of my things in storage in Lansing. I figured it's cheaper and easier than shipping it twice."

For a moment he didn't move. "What do you plan to do in the meantime?" His voice was husky, intense.

"I'm still working on that book I signed to do last year."

He looked perplexed. "I would've thought you'd be finished with the manuscript by now."

Susan grinned. "I should have been." It was a relief to talk about something impersonal, and she continued conversationally. "I've had a hard time gathering product information. Some of it, like the EPA ratings on car makes and models, has been hard to wade through. Obviously, I can't publish all of it, and it's been time-consuming to make selections. The manuscript was originally due in late September, but I was able to get a nine-week extension, so I've got until November seventh to finish it."

"Did you come up with a title yet?"

"A Guide to Living Single."

"I like that."

"Thanks." She'd forgotten how supportive Steve could be when he wanted. It felt good, talking to him again. If only they could be that cordial to one another all the time, she thought wistfully.

"Had any trouble writing the manuscript?"

He knew from previous talks that she'd had some reservations about switching from newspaper writing to book preparation. Susan shook her head. "None. It's coming along well. I hope to be finished ahead of schedule, but only time will tell."

"And after that?"

"I've already got videotapes of my work circulating at half the stations in the Midwest. I want to go back to television again. I have experience in the field now, so it shouldn't be quite as difficult to get hired somewhere. But jobs in the industry are still at a premium, so I'll have to go wherever the work is."

At the prospect of her leaving again, Steve seemed to bristle, but he kept his tone cordially light, uninvolved. "Any luck?"

"Not so far, no. But the book will keep me busy until I do get another position." Susan reflexively smoothed her skirt.

"Is that really what you want?" He seemed to be hoping she would tell him otherwise.

"Yes, it is." She paused, wanting him to understand. "I've worked hard to get as far as I have. I believe I can go a lot farther in the field of television journalism, but only if I make the necessary sacrifices."

"In other words, your personal life will have to continue to take a back seat to your ambition." Annoyance underscored his every word. His hands tightened over the steering wheel.

Despair washed over Susan. Remembering how he had hurt her by letting her down when the going had gotten tough, she said, "Only when I'm forced—unfairly, I might add—to make a choice." If only he hadn't been so remote when she'd been working in Michigan those first three months! If only he'd talked more, given more, she could have done the same. Instead, talking to him had been like talking to a brick wall. She had gotten that much of a response. Had he tried harder to be supportive then, their current situation might be so very different. They might even be going ahead with their original plans instead of quarreling about intrinsic parts of their personalities neither of them could change.

Steve said nothing in response to her veiled accusation. He merely opened the ticket book and began scribbling the date and time. "I still need to see some identification." His voice was casual but cool.

Susan wasn't sure what she had expected of him either when he'd called or now. A plea for friendship, a request for a date? But after all they had been to one another, it upset her to see him treat her as a stranger. Biting her lip hard in an effort to mask her hurt and confusion, she wordlessly handed over her driver's license. Steve remained silent. She watched as he recorded the number, state and her stated physical description, including hair color, eye color, age and height. Despite his careless manner, however, his handwriting was surprisingly legible.

"How long will you be staying in West Virginia?" he asked impersonally.

"I don't know," she revealed numbly in a tone that encouraged no more questions. "I hope no more than six months, but it could be as long as a year. It depends largely on how quickly I'm able to find another job."

Mouth compressed angrily, he tore off the ticket and handed it to her. She glanced at the notation. His official duty done, Steve stalked around the car and yanked open the door, as if unable to get rid of her quickly enough. Stunned by what she'd read, Susan stammered, "Wait a minute. What is this...fine?" Cool air reached her as she approached Steve, now standing near the curb.

"Three hours community service," he said crisply.

Anger raged through Susan, making her forget all else. What was this, some sort of extra duty for breaking his heart? "So I crossed the street without looking. I'm willing to pay the fine due me. As for working off the action physically, forget it." She brushed her hair from her face. "I'm not being put on any chain gang."

"You owe Grafton three hours of community service. You'll do it as ordered." His face was formidable and angry.

She took a deep breath and tried a more reasonable tact. "Steve, I don't have time for this." Surely they could put their differences aside and behave as rational adults? "I have a book to finish. I'm on a deadline."

"I couldn't care less about your book. I'm concerned with this community, period."

He had proved that in the past by choosing his role of sheriff over a life with her! She regarded him with disdain. "I object to what I consider very rude, illegal, unfair treatment!"

His teeth gleamed white in what was more a grimace than a smile. "If you want to argue with someone, Susan, tell it to the judge." He held up a silencing hand before she could protest. "I don't have the time or the energy to listen to your complaints." He quickly circled around the car and slid in behind the steering wheel. She watched in disbelief as he drove away.

Furious beyond words, Susan charged on home. The door slammed behind her as she entered the house. Thankfully, the guests for the reelection committee had not yet arrived. Her father glanced up from his evening paper. He was not one to spare his only daughter his opinion, and after greeting her, he observed, "That was quick. Your mother led me to believe you'd be out all evening."

She'd intended to be, but her rage at Steve had influenced her plans. Before she'd known it, she'd been turning up the walk to her home.

"Something wrong?" her father asked.

By his easy grin, she knew he'd heard Steve had called, wanting to see her, and probably guessed—correctly—that the Taylor County sheriff had managed to find her without too much trouble. And maybe, Susan guessed, a tip from her never-say-die mother. "I got a ticket!" She waved the yellow slip as evidence in front of her father.

Clayton Trent's brow furrowed. "For what?" As superintendent of schools, he and Steve had worked together often. The two men respected one another and got along well.

"Jaywalking!" Susan's cheeks felt as if they had been fueled with fire. In retrospect, the ticket was even more embarrassing.

Her father grinned and returned to his paper. "What's the fine? Community service? New thing around here. Haven't you noticed how clean and spruced up the town looks?"

Now that he mentioned it, Susan recalled Grafton had seemed inordinately tidy. "Steve does this to others?"

Her father nodded. "What's more, the townspeople approve, too."

"Well, I don't. I'm going to insist I be charged with a fine I can pay." In the back of her mind was the thought that if she could hold on to her outrage, she could somehow avoid the hurt.

Her father's brows lowered. Respect for the law was something he had drilled into her from the time she could talk. Again, he went back to his paper. "You can do that, Susan. But more than likely the judge won't hear of letting you off the hook."

"Why not?"

"Because there is no physical reason why you can't contribute to the care of the city. Things have changed around here since you left. The judge lets Steve figure out the fine for all misdemeanors, and because people are cash-short and time-rich, the fines are now doled out in community-service terms, across the board. It's a system that helps the community, helps the people and treats every one of the citizens fairly under the law. Work is work, or so they say. Of course the municipal judge has the power to disagree, but he never has yet. Saves us all a lot of time, as it happens. And taxes to boot. Plus, it has the advantage of making people think before and after they act.''

Her father was speaking like the school superintendent and educator he was. She couldn't argue about the merit of Steve's system, but it also had pitfalls— pitfalls her father, and others, seemed determined to ignore. "I can't believe this," she stated incredulously. "You're letting him run this town single-handedly!"

Her father agreed with a decisive nod. "Couldn't be a better, fairer man to do the job."

Susan groaned, cradling her head in her hands. It was backwoods thinking like that which had led her to city life. "That's monarchistic!"

"No, Susan," her father said serenely, smiling in the way that he did when an argument was over. "That's the new Grafton."

Chapter Two

At precisely six forty-five, Steve parked his Blazer in front of the Trents' home. Despite his efforts to put it out of his mind, he was still disturbed by the meeting with Susan. After switching off the jeep motor, he sat a moment longer, lost in a confused labryinth of crushed hopes and fond memories.

His mind drifted back to the first time they'd met. The party at the Winters' home had been noisy and crowded. But for him there had been only one woman in the room that night. His attraction toward Susan had been immediate and absolute. He had determined then that he would make her his, and he had. Yet from the beginning there had been difficulties, especially since she lived and worked more than two hundred and fifty miles away.

There'd been no doubt that she cared deeply for him. But her own ambition was stronger and probably always would be. He frowned, realizing that even then she'd been destined for something other than the ordinary. He supposed he had always known, deep down, that her star quality was in essence part of the strength of his attraction for her. Intellectually, he'd wanted success for her. Privately, personally, his thoughts had been another matter. He felt guilty as hell for wishing incessantly that just marriage to him would have been enough for the dynamic woman. But there was no changing what had happened any more than he could change Susan.

With an oath of frustration, he pushed from the jeep and began the short walk up to her front door. Emma Trent answered the door. She seemed unaccountably frazzled. He supposed it was due to having Susan home again, combined with the strain of entertaining after putting in a full day with her students. "Steve, I'm glad to see you." Emma sighed hugely. "I'm not nearly ready for guests."

"I suppose you know you've taken on too much?" he teased fondly, stepping into the front hall.

"So Clayton claims."

The amused gleam in Emma's eyes indicated that she, too, knew about the ticket. He muffled his own irritation. Delightful as Susan's mother was, her meddling could be irksome. This was one of those occasions. He knew she was thinking he'd given Susan a ticket out of spite or devilry. Saying it wasn't so, that Susan had almost gotten herself hit by a car, wouldn't help.

"Anything I can do to help?" he asked genially, skirting the obvious. Despite everything, Emma always made him feel welcome, like part of the family. Her warmth hadn't ended after the engagement had broken off.

"Yes. You can go upstairs and get Susan. I've called her twice, but she's not answering. I'd do it myself but—" She snapped her fingers in the direction of the kitchen as a buzzer hummed ominously in the background. "There's my microwave-oven timer. That means my brownies must be done. And I've got punch and sandwiches to make yet, too."

"Sure I can't pitch in and do whatever's necessary?" Steve asked. "I'd like to help."

"Certainly you can help," Emma said, smiling. "But I really need Susan, too."

"I'll get her," Steve promised. Dutifully, he headed for the stairs.

There was a reason for Susan's not answering, Steve discovered several moments later. Through the slightly open door he could see that Susan was curled up against the pillows on her bed. She had stereo headphones over her ears to block out noise. He rapped several times, but she remained oblivious to his presence, her concentration focused solely on whatever it was she was writing.

Exasperated, he crossed the room to her side, stopping just short of her canopy bed. Seeing him, she started, sat up and removed the headphones. Putting them aside, she reached over to switch off the stereo next to her bed.

"Your mother wanted me to tell you she needs your help."

Susan stretched, drawing the old and faded patchwork comforter around her. "I told her earlier I had no intention of involving myself in your campaign for reelection."

"Ever the optimist, your mother," Steve said lightly. His eyes dropped to the legal pad on her lap. From the looks of it, she'd already filled several pages with her bold scrawl. At the top of the page she'd been writing on was the heading Things to Do. "Getting organized?" he asked. He should have known she wouldn't waste any time getting busy again.

Susan nodded but stubbornly did not elaborate on her plans.

He grinned, vaguely amused and relieved to see her behaving so normally. He'd been worried about her when he'd learned of her release from WJCG. He saw now that she had bounced back with her customary determination. In fact, she'd probably emerge from this setback even stronger than she had been before.

The moment drew out awkwardly. "Well? What should I tell your mother?" Steve asked.

Susan sighed heavily. She tossed back the comforter, capped her pen and threw that aside, too. "Tell her I'll be right there."

She sounded annoyed. Steve shot her a sharp glance. "You don't have to do this for my sake."

About that much, evidently, they agreed. "But I do have to help my mother," Susan said calmly. Muttering an oath, she began looking around the floor. "I can't find my shoes." She sighed audibly again.

Reluctantly, Steve began looking, too. She'd only been back a couple of hours, and already her room was hopelessly cluttered with belongings. The hope chest at the bottom of her bed had been left open, as had several dresser drawers. Her vanity table was littered with cosmetic containers, shampoo and perfume. Her suitcases were strewn out over the floor, along with two open cardboard cartons of books and files, a portable typewriter and various office supplies.

"No wonder you can't find anything," Steve muttered, lifting up a garment bag draped over a chair. Beneath it were assorted stuffed animals left over from her childhood.

Susan knelt to look under the bed. "I told you I needed my own apartment." She pulled out an old baton and two dusty black tap shoes. "There's barely room enough for my old stuff here, aside from the luggage I brought with me."

"You won't get any argument there." Steve spotted what he thought was an old tennis shoe. It turned out to be some strangely fashioned arts and crafts project made with white canvas and red shoelaces. He had no idea what it was supposed to be.

"Give me that!" Susan snatched it from his hands. Her cheeks were flushed with embarrassment.

He grinned. "What is it?"

"Can't you tell? It's an urn."

"What?"

"Never mind." She sighed again. "Look in the closet, will you? I may have—"

Out of the corner of his eye he saw her pale as he started to turn toward her closet obediently. It was then that he saw the wedding dress. The meaning of the delicate white lace dress struck him forcefully. Never before that instant had he actually seen the wedding gown. He felt the color drain from his face. Anger swiftly replaced the discomfiture. His mouth compressed. "What the—"

"My mother's doing," she said faintly.

Moving swiftly past him, Susan shut the closet door. The wedding dress again out of sight, she seemed preoccupied with what might have been, what they would doubtless never have. In that instant, Steve felt sorry for them both. But she gave him no chance to console or share with her.

She turned away from him resolutely, lifted the coverlet on her bed and pulled out two bone-colored pumps, one after another. "Aha. I knew my shoes were here somewhere." She sat down, and crossing her legs, gracefully slipped them on.

Steve turned to go as she rolled down her shirt-sleeves and buttoned the cuffs at her wrists. "I'll tell your mother you're on your way down and give her a hand in the meantime."

"How many people are coming?" Susan asked, reaching for her suit jacket.

"Thirty, thirty-five." He gestured lamely. "I tried to talk her out of having refreshments."

"I know Mom. She wouldn't hear of it." Susan was all business. She slipped on her suit coat and reached for her hairbrush. "Tell Mom I'll be down in a minute. And don't just ask Dad to help. Persuade him and then hang around to see that he does. I don't want Mom getting overtired."

Steve nodded agreeably, grinning and shutting the door, the tension between them easing again as they both conspired to undo some of the burden on Susan's mother.

A minute later, her hair brushed, wrists scented with perfume, Susan was on her way downstairs. En route, she discovered Steve's sixteen-year-old brother, Eric. The lanky youth's face lit up when he saw her. "Susan, hi!"

Glancing past Eric, through the dining room, Susan could see that her mother now had plenty of help, not just from Steve and her dad but from several others, as well. Relaxing momentarily, Susan gave Eric an impulsive hug. "Hi, yourself, friend. How've you been?" Hands shoved into the pockets of his jeans, he looked like a younger, more wiry version of his older brother. Both had the same curly ash-blond hair, gorgeous eyes and sinewy strength. But where Steve was self-assured, serious and in control, Eric was adolescently frantic and hyperactive.

"Okay," Eric continued, grinning from ear to ear.

Susan directed him to a secluded spot just beneath the stairs. The living and dining room of her parents' rambling home was already filled with guests. "You look great."

"Thanks." Eric ducked his head shyly.

Susan sized him up, glad to see him looking so well. "As if you've grown another ten inches."

Eric flushed slightly. "Not quite that much."

"At least three."

"More like...four and a half."

Eric ducked his head and with the tip of his shoe nudged at a knothole on the parquet floor. Susan watched him wink at a pretty teenager across the room. The object of Eric's affections didn't return his admiring glance. "Who's the red-haired angel?" Susan asked lightly, sensing a very serious boy-girl interest there.

"Wendy Saunders. She's a cheerleader at the high school."

Dressed in fashionable clothes, Wendy was surrounded by several other youths who had accompanied their parents to help work on Steve's campaign. Eric seemed embarrassed by her lack of interest in him. Saving the moment, Susan linked arms with Eric and led him in the general direction of the kitchen. When his attention was again solely hers, she said, "How'd you get roped in to coming tonight?"

Politics and public appearances had never been Eric's forte. It said a lot about his regard for his brother that he wanted to be involved at all. "I thought it might be fun." Eric tugged uncomfortably at the collar of his plaid shirt. "And I want Steve to get what he wants."

"Even if it means living in Grafton?"

Having spent his early life in a suburb of New York City, Eric had never actively sought a rural life. Susan knew the two brothers had argued over it relentlessly in the past. "I guess." Eric paused. In a whisper, he confided, "Just between you and me, though, all this planning and campaigning seems like a waste of time. I mean, everybody knows how good Steve is, how dedicated. After the job he's done, who wouldn't want to vote for Steve?"

It was an idealistic view but one Susan privately shared. "Good point," she murmured. "Think if we voice it we'll get out of some work?" She laughed hopefully.

"Nope." Eric was sure of that much.

Susan laughed. Eric moved off to speak with some friends. Two minutes later, she found Steve in the kitchen, helping her mother and father put together a platter of sandwiches. He glanced up and saw Susan in the doorway, seeming even more at home there than she felt. It disconcerted her to find Steve every bit as capable as she in the melee. Not only had he continued to make himself comfortable in her absence, but he was apparently considered a member of the family by both Emma and Clayton Trent. No wonder her mother hung on to the wedding dress and her hope, Susan thought.

It was her father who organized the actual meeting. Everyone sat in the living room and formal dining room. "The way I see it," her dad started in the same genial but direct manner she imagined he used at school, "this election is vital to our town. The continued growth and prosperity of Grafton depends on having Steve Markham as sheriff. But it isn't going to be easy getting him reelected. In fact, the great job he has done clearing this town of corruption is going to make some people even more anxious to oust him. Among those people is Robert Wakefield, the son of Taylor County's ex-sheriff, Sheldon Wakefield." There was a murmur of horror and dissent among the group. Clayton continued. "The opposition will probably wring whatever sentiment they can from the voters by playing up the Wakefield tradition of law enforcement in all their political ads."

Steve shrugged off Clayton's worry offhandedly but couldn't hide the anxiety in his tone. He confronted others in the room. "In that respect, Robert may have one up on me. Although I've lived and worked here now for over four years, comparatively speaking, I am a newcomer to the area."

Unable to help herself, Susan countered angrily and defensively, "That's the only advantage Wakefield has on you. For heaven's sake, Steve, Robert's father was a crook! Do you think the people of Taylor County are going to forget that?"

Clayton quieted his daughter gently. "Honey, you know how some of the locals feel about outsiders. Wonderful as our current sheriff is—" Clayton sent Steve a sincere glance "—he is from New York. The Wakefield family, on the other hand, has resided in Grafton for generations. There are some who feel that Robert should have the job because his daddy once had it and his daddy before that."

Steve agreed grimly. Having been a deputy under the original Sheriff Wakefield for two years before challenging him for the position of sheriff, Steve knew just how corrupt and unfair the office had been. "Now that his father is dead, Robert figures people will forget how poor the Wakefields were at keeping law and order. Add to that, there have been rumors that the new food-processing plant here in town is considering backing Robert. Since they employ over three hundred and fifty local people, their support could lose the election for me."

"How so?" Susan asked.

Steve shrugged. "That depends on how they plan to show their support. If they contribute monetarily or sponsor ads in the paper or on radio or television, that certainly will hurt me. Because he already has a larger advertising budget than I do, thanks to his own financial resources."

Susan's brows furrowed. "Why would the new plant back Wakefield?" In the past, local industry had stayed out of county politics, refusing to endorse anyone, as had the papers.

Steve sighed. "Maybe because the management at the Lean Delight factory is new and doesn't know the Wakefield law-avoidance legacy."

"And maybe they've been paid off or promised favors in return," Eric said bitterly.

Susan turned. Steve said nothing. She could tell by the expression on his face that he felt the same was true, but she knew him well enough to realize he would never accuse anyone of anything, either publicly or privately, unless he first had indisputable facts and proof of the alleged deed. Tension radiated in the room.

"The question is, Susan," Clayton Trent countered, beaming down at her as he just had at Steve, "how do we best represent Steve in the campaign so that the voters of Taylor County will not only remember what he has accomplished but vote for him again regardless of who's formally endorsed. After all, once one steps into the voting booth, the matter is strictly private."

"However it is accomplished, it must be done without slinging mud," Steve interjected. "The last thing I want to do is hash out past injustices and rile people up again."

Susan respected him for that. Especially, she thought amusedly, since there was nothing many West Virginians loved more than a good argument. A spirited one could go on for days with the people involved often forgetting the real issues.

"Concentrate on what you've done for the community since taking office," Susan suggested.

Emma stood, reaching for the coffeepot on the dining-room table. Finding it nearly empty, she started again for the kitchen. "Maybe you should be the one to write the copy, Susan."

"You do have a journalism degree," her dad added.

"And the polish of someone used to working with the media," said another.

Susan half expected Steve to bail her out, to appoint someone else. He didn't, instead, he waited, his eyes clashing with hers, as if inwardly he was speculating about her answer. "Unless you think the job is too much for you," Steve said finally.

Susan bristled. "Of course I can handle it."

"Good. Then the job is yours," Susan's father finished, not giving her a chance to debate further. A born manager, Clayton Trent was never happier than when everything was settled and progress under way. "Delbert's Printing has already agreed to make up posters and bumper stickers for cost."

The chatter went on. An hour later, a bewildered and exhausted Susan stepped out onto the back porch for air. She'd come home for peace, quiet and rest and found herself at the heart of what looked to be a very busy political campaign. Minutes later, Steve joined her. "You don't have to accept the position, you know," he said softly. "I realize the committee put you on the spot."

Darkness surrounded them. Despite her sweater, Susan shivered in the cool evening air. "Don't be silly. I'm the logical person for the position. Besides, I believe in your ability to do the job, Steve." That was what had made her leaving and accepting the job in Lansing so hard—that he was so committed to what he did. If only the position of sheriff had been just a job to him and not a heartfelt commitment to the community, it would have been so much easier to ask him to go with her.

"I'd understand if you wanted to back out." He was standing just in front of her.

She thought of how easily her feelings for him were sparking to life again. Being with him again would be treacherous. "I'm sure you can understand why I wouldn't want to work closely with you, Steve, after all that's happened, but I doubt anyone else in the community would. They'd think it was sour grapes on my part."

His hand caught her wrist when she moved to step past him, toward the house. "I don't want your help unless it's what you want, too, Susan." He held her arm against his chest. Beneath the deceptively casual grip, she could feel the tension coiled within him and the steady beat of his heart.

Susan swayed against him. Old conflicts and emotions were beginning to surface. She fought against becoming emotionally preoccupied either with him or his campaign. "I'll help you. But I'm doing it as a friend. I don't want to get involved again."

His resentment flashed between them like a bolt of lightning. "Who said I did?" he demanded incredulously, before she could so much as take a breath. "Just because I phoned you this afternoon...to see how you were, if there was anything I could do...in light of your unemployment." He paused. "You take a lot for granted, Susan. You always did."

She stared at him. He couldn't have shocked her more if he had announced he was engaged to an ape. Was he trying to tell her that his feelings for her had come to a dead end? If so, he could have found a less public place and time to do it. "And you didn't take a lot for granted?" she retorted.

"I guess I did." His uncivil tone made it clear it wasn't a mistake he intended to make again.

There was another moment's waiting, and then he released her. Feeling her composure crumble under the scrutiny of his lancing gaze, she stepped backward. Her fingers curled around the porch railing behind her. Even with the wood for support, she felt no more steady.

"All right," he said softly, dangerously. "We'll do it your way for now." Voices from inside buzzed louder. She heard her name called, then Steve's. The back door slammed. Her mother came out on the porch.

"Oh, here you are," Emma exclaimed. Seeing the two of them alone, she reached again for the back door, as if preparing to immediately go back inside the house.

Susan told her, "You don't have to run off, Mom. You're not interrupting anything." She had promised herself when she decided to go back to Grafton that she wouldn't let him hurt her again, and she had meant it. Maybe that was part of the reason why she had come back, too—to prove he no longer had the power.

"Nothing except maybe the beginning of a good fight," Steve remarked lazily.

Susan glowered at Steve. Emma laughed, shaking her head. "Susan, it's good to have you home."

Susan felt so, too. But just how Steve really felt, she didn't know. Judging from his reserved behavior during the evening, she figured it would be a long time, if ever, before she did find out.

Chapter Three

The group that asesmbled Saturday morning on the limestone courthouse steps for community-service duty was a varied one. There was Gena Borden, a brash former adversary and ex-schoolmate of Susan's. "Well, if it isn't the Sweetheart of Grafton High," Gena observed laconically as Susan joined the group. She held a cigarette pinched between her thumb and first finger. "What are you doing here, Susan? Or would you prefer I didn't ask—at least not in front of everyone else?" Gena smoked incessantly and had a knack for reading Susan's feelings with deadly accuracy.

Steve looked up from his clipboard, and watching the exchange between the two women with pensively narrowed eyes, said nothing to interfere.

"I, uh, got picked up for jaywalking," Susan mumbled, red-faced. Built like a tank, with a you-can-bet-I'll-never-say-die glare in her eyes, Gena was tough, capable of physically taking on and maybe even beating any man there, including Steve. In the past, Susan had always been half afraid of her, and that much hadn't changed. Gena and she had always seemed to operate on two different planes of experience; apparently they still did. Susan backed up slightly, taking without comment the plastic garbage bag Steve handed her. "What are you here for, Gena?"

Gena shot Steve an amused glance. Abruptly, she seemed not to mind the least bit taking her punishment. "A drunk and disorderly charge. I got a little rowdy the other night." Steve struggled with a grin and continued writing, his eyes downcast.

"I was arm wrestling with some of the guys from the mines," Gena continued affably.

"Gena won, too." Deputy Frank Winter commented. Steve gave him a look that effectively cut off the rest of the story.

Gena accepted the credit due her with an unabashed glance and a shrug of her hefty shoulders. She grinned broadly. "That's when the fight started. The guy didn't want to pay up."

"Gambling is illegal, Gena," Steve said without looking up.

"Uh...right." Gena corrected, loudly enough for everyone in the group to hear. "Money they owed me for...yard work," she lied. Eyes gleaming, she dared Steve to confront her. To Susan's surprise, Steve only grinned back wryly and kept writing. There was a rumble of appreciative laughter from the group. In addition to Susan and Gena, Steve and his deputy, there were also two teens. They were apparently doing time for vandalism charges. "Next time you soap windows," Steve said, giving them two buckets, a bundle of rags and a bottle of ammonia, "make sure it's for cleaning purposes only." Two feuding neighbors, involved in a property-line dispute, were also present. Not speaking at all to one another, they were uncooperative and required constant supervision by Steve and his deputy. Painstakingly, the crew swept the courthouse steps and raked the surrounding tree-covered grounds free of fallen leaves and debris.

Gena and Susan were soon busy picking up bits of garbage from the main lawn. Susan was amazed to find how much litter could accumulate. "So how long are you going to stay?" Gena asked at last. Surprisingly, once they were off a way from the others, Gena adapted a half-friendly tone.

Susan shrugged. "I don't know. Six months, maybe." They moved steadily down the street. Susan bent to pick up a crushed paper cup and mangled straw. Aware that Steve was now within earshot, she continued. "I rented a furnished apartment over on East Grove Street."

"Moving in soon?" Gena asked. She picked up a half-empty package of cigarettes and examined the damp contents before tossing them into the litter bag with a reluctant sigh.

"Officially, Monday, though I've brought some essentials over and had the utilities turned on. I'll be painting it later today and tomorrow." She wouldn't be able to sleep there until after the paint smell had vanished.

Gena nodded. After a moment, she moved away, no longer interested in forced chitchat. Susan concentrated on her work. She had dressed down for the occasion, wearing ancient Levi's and a thigh-length shirt garnered from the back of her father's closet. If

Steve's frequent glance was any indication, though, he found nothing lacking in her attire.

The morning dragged on. Several hours later, her back was aching, Susan was tired and out of sorts. Steve was right about one thing, she mused irritably. She would never jaywalk again. Nor would she ever litter. Not that she ever had.

A low, long wolf whistle caught Susan's attention. She cringed, then turned when it sounded again. Straightening, Susan looked around curiously. The *Taylor County Bugle* editor, Patsy Winter, focused a Nikon Susan's way. A click of the shutter later, Susan and the others working on the courthouse steps had been immortalized on film. Susan swore, low and furiously.

"Why did you do that?" Susan demanded, covering her tousled hair with her hand as a laughing Patsy sauntered closer. "I thought we were friends." During high school, the two of them had been inseparable.

Patsy stopped to give her husband, Frank, a kiss. Petite and slender, she was covered with freckles from head to toe. "Didn't you know?" Patsy teased. "The picture session is de rigueur with those that get caught working off fines on Saturday mornings. We print their pictures as regularly as we print DWI charges."

Susan groaned. "Just what I need." No wonder her father had been so amused. Undoubtedly, he had known how she would take such publicity.

"Seriously, Susan," Patsy continued, "aren't you about done here for the day?" Patsy looked hopefully at Steve for confirmation.

Susan glanced at her watch, then at Steve. From his perch high on the courthouse steps, he nodded. "Yeah."

"Look, why not come have lunch with me, then," Patsy persuaded, linking arms with Susan. "You look like you need a break. It would give us a chance to get caught up. My mom has the kids for the afternoon, so I've got the time, if you do."

Patsy worked full-time and managed a rambunctious brood of five children. The two women had been given precious little time to spend alone and simply chat in the years since graduation. "That sounds heavenly," Susan agreed. "Just let me get rid of the trash."

Twenty minutes later, Susan was seated in Patsy's office at the newspaper. Feet propped up on chairs, both were enjoying thick juicy cheeseburgers and fries from the hamburger emporium down the street. "So tell me, how goes it on the *Taylor County Bugle*?" Susan asked.

Patsy grimaced, dabbing the corner of her mouth with a napkin. "Well, you know the paper has never produced a financial windfall. But since Daddy died, it has been getting progressively harder to make the *Bugle* stay in business, especially with the rising costs of home delivery, labor, paper, ink. You name it, everything has gone up drastically except the price the average patron is able or willing to pay for the yearly subscription."

"I'm sorry." Susan's sentiment was genuine.

Patsy shrugged. "As they say, that's business, and I can weather whatever happens. At the moment, Frank and I make enough to get by and take care of the children. And as long as we're able to do that, I'll keep the *Bugle* open and running, because I think it does provide an excellent community service. But if we don't find a way to increase the avertising, we may have to fold by the end of the year.

"In some ways I'd be glad to let the old dinosaur die. And in other ways, when I think of my daddy starting this business on a shoestring and keeping it going all those years..." Patsy grew silent. Only because of their close friendship had Patsy confided that much, Susan knew.

"Is there anything I can do to help?" Susan asked. She had the distinct feeling Patsy wanted to ask her something but was hesitant, not wanting to use their friendship presumptuously to business advantage. "Maybe I could write some articles. Or do some of the routine stories while I'm here," Susan suggested. "I worked for the paper summers during college."

"I don't think I can afford you, Susan," she said cautiously.

"For heaven's sake, Patsy. I meant I'll do them for free."

"No." Patsy's lower lip quivered. Old friends or not, she would not accept charity.

"Scale, then," Susan bartered.

Patsy paused. "Maybe. If you can come up with something that excites you." As they finished their lunch, they talked about Susan's plans for the future, her desire to go back into television and the book she was working on. Patsy brightened. "I know you...hate publicity, Susan. And that this is not a particularly stellar time of your life. But you are a celebrity to many of the people here."

Susan knew what was coming. Warily, she asked, "You want to do an article on me?"

"Front page." Patsy said bluntly. "Would you mind?"

"I think I owe you one."

They talked for the next hour, Patsy interviewing Susan on what had been happening in her life and how it felt to work in television, the pros and cons, and her plans for the future. When Susan left, it was with the knowledge that her photo would be on the front page of the next edition of the *Bugle*.

She had no sooner returned to her apartment and opened a can of creamy beige paint when the doorbell rang. She opened the apartment door to see Steve and Eric Markham standing on her doorstep. Both wore old paint-splattered jeans and worn sweatshirts. "Need some help?" Eric asked, grinning.

"Doesn't look to me like she's even started," Steve observed. Hands in his pockets, he leaned against the door frame and thoughtfully looked over the interior of her apartment before turning back to her.

Her surprise at seeing the two Markham brothers on her doorstep faded somewhat. Susan adjusted the brim of the painter's cap lower over her eyes. "You're right. I haven't started," Susan shot back much more amiably than she felt, her eyes never leaving Steve's face. "And yes," she continued cautiously, unable to think of a way to refuse the men's offer without hurting Eric's feelings, "I could use whatever help you men could give me." She cast an appreciative look at Eric, pointedly ignoring Steve. She still hadn't quite forgiven him for the community-service fine, even though she knew she had deserved the citation.

Eric, however, seemed oblivious to the tension between Susan and Steve. "Got some extra paintbrushes?" Eric asked, inspecting the paint and the surfaces Susan had been about to cover.

Susan forced a smile, glad to be able to concentrate on something else. "The brushes are in the kitchen. I'll get them."

Eric stayed in the living room. To her dismay, Steve followed Susan, watching as she extracted an extra paintbrush and roller from the brown hardware-store bag on the counter.

He was careful not to crowd her. "I hear you're going to be the featured story in next week's edition of the *Taylor County Bugle*." His words were laced with irony.

Susan glanced over at him, unable to prevent the warmth of a blush from flooding her cheeks. "How did you know?" Her lips pursed wryly.

"Frank, Patsy's husband, told me what she had in mind after the two of you went off to lunch." He continued softly. "It just stands to reason, because of your friendship and the *Bugle*'s current fiscal difficulties, that you would agree to help make at least one sellout edition."

She found herself pleased at his unexpected approval. "Well, not to worry," Susan said lightly, embarrassed. "The article won't be without its humanizing touch. Patsy plans to run the photo of me cleaning up the community right alongside the airbrushed publicity shot WJCG sent out."

"I'm sure both pictures will look great," Steve said tactfully.

"Thanks." Susan flushed again.

Recalling her vow to remain uninvolved, she forced herself to concentrate on organizing the trio. Like it or not, her apartment had to be painted to be truly livable, and she hadn't relished the thought of doing the chore alone. After some thought on how to proceed most efficiently, she said, "Steve, you get the ladder and the roller and do the high spots, near the ceiling and over the windows and doors, please. I'll do the trim. And Eric, you can do all the low areas in between."

After some initial clowning around, they worked in relative silence. Eventually, Susan asked, "So, Eric, do you want to tell me how this all came about? Whose idea was it?"

Eric grinned, all too willing to confess. "Your mom hinted the other night before you came down that you might be needing some help when it came time to move in to whatever apartment you decided to rent Steve and I saw her in the supermarket last night. She always buys her groceries on Friday evening, too. She said you were planning to paint today. It just seemed natural enough for us to help, especially when she mentioned you wouldn't let her or your dad do it because of their arthritis." Eric took a deep breath, pausing to put his paintbrush down. "Steve offered to call and ask if you wanted help, but your mom said not to, that you'd probably just refuse if we did and that it would be better just to show up, ready to work." Eric was delighted to be a part of any family conspiracy.

Susan looked at Steve. Her heart sank as she realized this was mostly her mother's doing.

Steve frowned. Cautiously, he elaborated on Eric's narrative. "We owe your mom a lot of home-cooked dinners."

Her spirits sank a little at that, but she remained upbeat. "Well, whatever the reason you came, I'm very glad you did. You were really helpful." She turned back to Eric. "Though I insist on paying you." Susan might not have had much pin money right then, but Eric certainly had less. And since he was old enough to date, he probably needed every penny he could get.

"You don't need to pay either of us," Steve interjected firmly, to Eric's undisguised dismay.

Susan sensed by the firm set of his lips that it wasn't a battle she would win with Steve, no matter how long she argued with him. She relented graciously. "How about dinner, then. We'll have Eric's favorite. I'll spring for a take-out pizza with everything."

"All right with me," Eric said.

Steve nodded. "Pizza sounds fine. But we'll split the cost." He pulled out his wallet before Susan could protest. "I owe you for the work you're going to do on my campaign."

Susan sighed. "There's no arguing with you, is there?"

Steve paused to wipe his hands on a paper towel he'd stuck into his belt, then moved the ladder to a spot farther toward the left. "Not on this, or we won't stay to eat."

"Stop arguing, Susan, please!" Eric pleaded swiftly, clasping both hands in front of him and sinking to his knees.

Realizing Eric's intensity was probably firmly grounded, Susan laughed. "What's the matter? Doesn't he feed you enough junk food?" She gave Steve a playful glance, startled to discover how dark and intent his eyes could be. The muscles in his back and shoulders rippled as he painted.

Eric grumbled expansively, "He feeds me enough broccoli and brussels sprouts to grow them out of my ears!"

"You're still growing. You need your vitamins." Steve gave his brother a playful mock punch to the shoulder, then wordlessly pointed out a spot Eric had missed. "Get back to work, kid."

"We'll have pizza as soon as we're finished," Susan promised. Steve climbed back up his ladder.

The next hours passed quickly. For a while it was like old times, with the three of them laughing and talking and working on a joint project. All too soon, the walls were finished. Eric was starving and ready to eat. "My phone has yet to be installed, so you'll have to go down to the pizza place and order there," Susan said. Reaching into her pocket, she impulsively tossed him the car keys. "You can take my car." Seeing Steve was about to object, she said, "Come on. It's only three blocks. After all the work Eric has put in here this afternoon, he deserves a little fun."

Steve, however, seemed to think it was not a good idea to put Eric behind the wheel of any Mazda. No less a shiny red RX-7. Sensing it would be useless to argue with Susan, he said finally, "Be careful. No speeding."

"Yes, sheriff." Eric grinned and walked out the door.

"And don't get paint on the interior!" Susan shouted, following him to the window.

"I won't." Eric spun around for proof. Miraculously, he had nary a drop on him. Susan and Steve were both covered with smudges.

"You spoil him," Steve chided after Eric drove away.

"And you worry too much," she responded, reveling in the feeling of closeness their joint work session had fostered. Steve nodded, as if distracted. She touched his arm lightly, tilting her face up to his. "Steve? What is it?"

For a second, she didn't think he would respond. Finally, he said, "Eric's been hanging out with this group of kids. A bunch of car fanatics; they all drive fancy cars and wear clothes that cost more than I can afford. That girl Wendy is part of the group, though, like Eric, she's still on the fringes. Eric wants to but can't compete with them, financially or otherwise. And frankly I don't want him to. So far, he's been accepted because he has a way with cars and can fix a lot of minor problems just by tinkering. He's bought every car manual available. You know, he feels he has more in common with the kids in that group than he does with some of the miners' and tobacco farmers' kids. I can sympathize with that. What does he know about raising a calf or being in the local chapter of 4-H?"

"You've given Eric the best upbringing you can," Susan said softly, fiercely. "You've taken on a burden many other men would have shirked."

"I'm not so sure that when it comes to being a parent just trying hard is enough." Steve rubbed a paint smudge from his jaw. He hadn't realized until that moment how much he'd missed having Susan to confide in on a daily basis. His eyes searched hers and found only compassion and understanding. "I thought I'd be able to give him a more stable life here than in the city. I felt there was less trouble for an adolescent to get into. But my reasons were selfish, too. I like living here, Susan. To me environment is everything, and the Blue Ridge Mountains are more than likely the closest I'll ever get to living in paradise. I like being a stone's throw from white water and rugged terrain, fishing for brook trout whenever the mood strikes me instead of just on vacation once a year." *And most of all,* Steve thought, *I love being here with you, Susan.* But her feelings toward him had changed. And as such, he had to think about his brother. Steve continued, crossing his arms protectively. "Eric hates it here, Susan. He hasn't said much, but I have a gut feeling he hates even the idea of my running for re-election."

"Then why would he help with the campaign?"

Steve shrugged dismissively. "How would it look if he didn't? He doesn't want to hurt my feelings any more than I want to hurt his. But the fact remains that like you and me, Eric and I want different things out of life." Susan winced at the vague reference to their breakup. Steve could have kicked himself for making the comparison. He continued more cautiously. "I took him back to the city last summer for a visit. He wanted to stay in New York, finish his senior year at a high school there, live at the home of one of his friends. I wouldn't let him because I know in my heart it's not what our parents would have wanted for him.

They would have wanted us to stay together at least until Eric was eighteen.''

"And Eric doesn't understand that?'' Her initial response was to reach over and hold him close. But their past differences kept her rooted firmly in place.

Steve rubbed the back of his neck, as if that would dispel some of the parental-fraternal anxiety he was feeling. It had been hard for him being both sibling and parents to his younger brother, Susan knew. Yet no one could fault him for lack of effort. Whenever Eric had needed him, Steve had been there. "Eric is a kid. He knows what he wants and goes after it. He's not at the point where he thinks things through. Sure, he wants to go now. He sees all the concerts available to him there, the hipness of the street scene. He doesn't know what the flip side would be like. I don't want him to find out about crime and pollution first-hand. I don't want him homesick. I don't want to lose him. He's all the family I've got.'' Steve's hands knotted into fists. His voice was low, anguished.

"What does Eric say now?'' she asked gently. Steve had never been one to talk much about his feelings. He felt deeply, but he didn't discuss much. For him to have confided in her that much, so soon, meant the situation with his brother was really bothering him.

His eyes caught hers for an ominously long moment. Susan read his frustration, and her heart went out to him as he continued. "Eric stopped talking about the possibility weeks ago, but I have the feeling he still hasn't quite forgiven me for forbidding him to live there.''

"Is that what all the razzing about too many vegetables is about?" Susan asked intuitively. It felt good to be with Steve again, to be sharing.

Steve nodded. "He thinks I'm overprotective."

"Are you?"

Steve took a deep breath. "Hell, yes." He gestured expansively. "After losing my parents," *and my fiancée,* he thought, "I don't want to lose him, too."

She took several steps nearer. "Eric is sixteen. He'll be leaving home in another few years, anyway. And by then he'll understand your decision."

He nodded perfunctorily. "Try not to worry," she said gently, impulsively taking his hand between her own.

"Thanks for being interested," Steve said.

Throat dry, Susan nodded, then disengaged her hand. If he was aware of her powerful response to him, he didn't show it. Oddly, his nonreaction made her feel worse rather than better.

Together they walked into the kitchen. Susan removed the painter's cap shielding her hair and raked her fingers through the glossy length, feeling ridiculously scruffy with paint dotting her arms, shirt and trousers. "How is it I got more paint on me than you did on you?" she teased. Steve couldn't seem to keep his eyes off her.

"Gravity," he remarked. "I was standing on a ladder. All drips run down the wall, not on clothes."

"Depends on who's handling the brush or roller," Susan murmured. She managed to get paint on her no matter where or how she worked. Finding his intense scrutiny more disconcerting than her private thoughts, she flashed a reluctant smile, then turned to rummage for dinnerware and paper plates in the cupboard. "Eric ought to be back soon. It probably wouldn't hurt to set the table."

"How can I help?" Hands resting loosely on his waist, he watched her set the necessary items on the counter and remove ice cubes from the trays.

"Clear off the table."

"Done." Five minutes later, the table was set, the drinks poured.

In a less than subtle attempt to change the subject, he looked around the apartment. Located on the first floor of a subdivided house, the one-bedroom apartment included a combination living-dining room and kitchen and a small but cozy bath. "This is nice," he commented. "Furniture all come with it?"

Susan nodded. "I'm having some boxes of towels, linens and kitchenware sent down from Lansing next week. I'm leaving everything else in storage. Earlier today I brought over basic groceries and all necessary items like paper towels, soap and tissues."

He nodded. "If you need any help—" This time the invitation came completely of his own volition, without prompting.

She smiled, the distance between them seeming to grow smaller. "Thanks."

He nodded, his eyes still holding hers.

The slamming of the front door marked Eric's return. Steve and Susan relaxed simultaneously. Eric sprinted in, carrying a pizza box in his hands. He looked unbearably excited. "Something happen on the way to the pizza place?" Steve asked. Susan caught his glance and smiled. For a second they were like two proud parents.

"As a matter of fact—" Eric paused hopefully, unable to suppress his enthusiasm "—I've got a date."

"For tonight?" Steve queried.

Eric nodded, practically holding his breath until Steve reluctantly gave his younger brother official permission and reflexively folded money into Eric's hand for the date. Eric thanked him and shoved the bills into his pocket. "You've got time to eat, I hope," Susan said.

Eric looked longingly toward the pizza Susan was doling out. He was a current of hyperkinetic energy. "Much as I'd like to stay, I, uh, promised Wendy I'd be there in an hour. Don't worry, we'll get something before the movie." He laughed, then shook his head as if unable to believe his good luck. "I've been trying to get her to go out with me for weeks now. But no luck." He raised his hands, palms up, as if to acknowledge facetiously his own worth. "All of a sudden she's interested." Without skipping a beat, he backstepped toward the door. "Steve, I need the Blazer. I've gotta run home, shower, shave, change." Steve sighed and tossed him the jeep keys.

Eric paused. "How will you get home?"

"Don't worry," Susan said, glad to help out Eric in any way she could. "I'll manage your brother's transportation home."

Eric's mind was only on his date. "Would you? Gee, thanks, Susan. I knew I could count on you." He was out the door and around the corner of the apartment house before his brother could speak.

Susan laughed and glanced over at Steve.

Having lost command of the situation so suddenly, he looked shaken. As if still stunned, he didn't say a word in reference to their unexpected change in plans.

She fought hard to hide her amusement. "Well, sheriff," she drawled sweetly, handing him a paper napkin, paper plate with pizza and a glass of soda, "it looks like you're at my mercy...again."

Chapter Four

"I never minded being at your mercy, Susan."

She heard the irony in his voice, mingling with desire. His masculine aura filled the room with a presence that was as sensually intimidating as it was alluring. "So I recall." Now it was her turn to want to run.

His smile was gradual. He fixed his gaze on her. Never the easily excited type, Susan nonetheless felt a definite weakness in her knees. Paint fumes, she thought. The smell is making me light-headed. But even as she thought it, she knew the frantic assumption was far from the truth.

She wasn't indifferent to him, Steve thought triumphantly. No matter how much she wanted to put the love they'd had safely out of reach, she couldn't do it any more than he could. Still, she struggled visibly against surrender. "You don't think we should be seeing each other again?" His voice was faint beneath the difficult question. With effort, he kept a damper on his own resentment. He didn't want her to fight either of them; he wanted her to give in. Unequivocally. Now.

She recognized again his uncanny ability to intuit what was on her mind. It took her a moment to regain her equanimity. She used the time to carry their supper to the table. "I'm not sure where it can lead." She should never have invited him for dinner or offered to drive him home when Eric declared he needed the Blazer.

"Because you're leaving again." His look was direct and uncompromising.

"Yes." His intimate knowledge of her gave him a certain power. She didn't like his method of turning the tables to regain the upper hand. Where he was concerned, she would have much rather have been in control, calling all the shots, setting the pace of their meetings. It was safer. Now it was she who felt at his mercy. With a sigh, she sat down at the table. Her provocative remark moments earlier had been issued involuntarily. She was hurt because he seemed so damn reluctant to either stay alone with her or accept a ride back to his place. But there was no changing that now. Whatever reservations he'd initially felt seemed to have faded. In their place came an intent as old and sensually identifiable as mankind. She would just have to fight him and herself as best she could.

Steve took the seat not opposite her but next to her. His leg brushed hers slightly as he sat down. She shifted her knees until they touched again.

"I agree we'll never be friends." Susan looked up at Steve, startled by his assertive tone. "There's always been too much feeling between us for anything lukewarm, Susan," he continued. But he knew now he wanted her back. And he was willing to work on her endlessly to see that his wish turned into reality. Her continued nervousness was a good sign. It confirmed she still felt something.

Susan looked down at her pizza. Her appetite had diminished. Desperate to change the subject and the focus of his attention, she turned her thoughts to his own life. "Where are you living now?" When Susan had left Grafton, he'd been staying in a rented house near the outskirts of town.

"I bought a small farm about six miles out. Eric and I have been working on the place."

Casually, she spread a napkin across her lap. "What kind of shape is it in?"

"At the moment it looks kind of homespun. When I bought it, it was run down. The only thing good about it was the frame. We had to have it rewired, new plumbing put in. Eric and I installed new drywall. Last spring we sanded and refinished the floors, put down new linoleum in the kitchen."

"How large is it?"

"Eighteen hundred square feet. Three bedrooms upstairs, and a bath. Downstairs, we have a kitchen, dining room, living room and small den. When you drive me home, you can come in and see it. I'd be interested in your opinion." He braced his elbows on the table edge.

"Steve—" She wanted him to stop trying to pick up where they had left off, as if nothing had happened.

"Don't trust me?" His brows arched. He grinned, saying very low, "Maybe you shouldn't."

"Maybe I won't." The more he pushed, the easier it was to dig in her heels and resist. Maintaining distance was best for both of them, she reminded herself sternly.

He grinned again in response. She carried her plate to the kitchen. Steve was right behind her, his strides long and lazy. As she reached the kitchen sink, his low, beguiling voice murmured against her neck. "Hold on a second." His hand lifted to her hair.

"What is it?" Susan turned toward him, her back against the sink, her hands grasping the countertop on either side of her. Her voice was husky but controlled.

Saying nothing, he closed the last of the distance between them amiably. His hand cupped the back of her neck. He tilted her head slightly to the right. As she moved, his other hand came up to lift several strands of her hair. "You've got paint right here. A nice bit of ecru amid all that glossy dark brown."

Susan hissed regretfully. Perdition. "I thought wearing a cap would prevent that. Is it bad?"

He contemplated how to answer her. He liked her having to depend on him, even for a second. His low teasing laugh sounded through the apartment. She looked more apprehensive. Shrugging, he said, "Depends on how much you like looking different from everyone else. Don't worry. The paint is water base. It should wash right out. In fact, I think I can get rid of most of it by combing through your hair." Before she could stop him, he drew a small comb from the back pocket of his jeans. They were standing very close. His thigh pressed against hers as he lifted a strand of hair. Holding it aloft between his fingers, he gently tugged the comb through—once, then again and again. Minuscule paint flakes fell to her shoulders. With the same velvet efficiency, he brushed, then blew them away.

"How's it coming?" Susan detested the faint breathlessness of her voice. His touch surrounded her with sensual memories it would have been much safer to forget.

The humorous note had left his voice. "Almost out." He reached for a paper towel near the sink, switched on the water and dampened it. Deftly, using only the edge of the dampened towel, he rinsed the remaining paint from her hair, then patted it dry. Steve was lost in his own absorbing memories. Impossible as it seemed, Steve thought, he'd forgotten just how softly yielding she could be, how very vulnerable. The warmth of her gilded him in a wealth of sensations more pleasurable than gold, more enticing that he could ever have remembered or anticipated. He knew she was aware of his arousal. Her own breathing was erratic. He could see the pulse thrumming rapidly in her throat.

Susan pushed away from him, every nerve ending alive.

Surprisingly, Steve made no effort to pursue her. Wordlessly, he cleared the table of paper plates and glasses. Susan wrapped the leftover pizza in foil and put it in the refrigerator. I've got to stop letting him get to me, she told herself.

So she was still skittish, he thought. That didn't surprise him. Nor did it deter him. But for the moment he would go easy. He'd give her time to adjust to being with him again. He wouldn't forfeit the rest of the evening, especially when she'd already pledged to help with his campaign. "When do you want to work on my biography for the campaign brochures?" he asked calmly.

Susan looked taken aback. After a moment, she shrugged. "Tonight would be all right, I guess."

"Want to go to my place?" He'd gone to Susan's reluctantly, feeling trapped by Eric's and Emma's maneuvering but knowing he owed much to the Trent family. He hadn't expected to feel so attracted to her. He hadn't expected to feel so far apart, as if they were in many ways farther apart emotionally than ever before, yet tied to one another through the past just the same. It was a hell of a sensation, wanting her the way he did, physically, emotionally, yet feeling perpetually pushed away by Susan. "With Eric out for the evening, it would be quiet."

Too quiet. "I'd rather work at my parents' home. It'll be easier and more efficient because my stuff is still in boxes. We can use my mother's typewriter in the den."

Her undisguised efforts to keep him at arm's length both amused and annoyed him. "She won't mind us traipsing in unannounced?" He half hoped Emma had planned some huge social event there that would make staying impossible.

The lines around his eyes deepened as he smiled, still watching her reactions. "Mind?" Susan repeated, barely able to choke back her laughter. "My mother will be delighted to have us drop by together," she finished dryly. Emma would also act as a chaperone, something Susan needed. Maybe if Steve saw she wasn't so anxious to climb right back into his bed, he'd cool his advances to a more manageable degree, Susan decided. "And as enthusiastic as my parents are about your campaign, I'm sure they'll gladly loan us the use of my mother's reconditioned IBM for one night.''

''Your parents' home it is, then,'' Steve conceded.

The drive to the Trent house was accomplished in relative silence. Susan was all too aware of Steve in the passenger seat. His tall, masculine frame seemed to fill the sporty car to overflowing. More disconcerting still, during the ride he never took his eyes off her profile. His face gave away nothing, Susan noted peripherally as they paused at a traffic light, but his eyes glittered with quiet contemplation.

Recalling how unsupportive he had been of her work at a time when she had needed him most, she refused to give in to the inner demands being with him again was generating. She was cool, almost aloof, as they mounted the steps to her parents' eighty-year-old home. They would do this as two professionals, she determined willfully, two uninvolved old friends who just happened to be on the same political side.

Unfortunately, Emma and Clayton didn't see Susan and Steve's joint appearance with the same perspective. They not only offered Susan and Steve use of the den, but promptly vacated the premises, promising not to return until well after midnight. Desperate to detain her ''chaperones,'' Susan said, ''Don't you want to help us work on the brochures?''

Emma and Clayton exchanged glances. ''We're sure you can handle it, honey,'' Clayton said finally, turning back to his daughter. ''Besides, your mother and I have been planning to see this movie for weeks. We just didn't realize the feature was playing in Clarksburg until a few minutes ago.''

A likely story. If it wouldn't have looked as if she were running, Susan would have suggested that both she and Steve accompany the Trents. A double date, with her parents cheering her on, might be worse than a rakishly stalking Steve. Damn it, Susan decided, she could handle Steve. All she had to do was keep him at arm's length.

Resignedly, Susan waved her parents off a moment later. The door closed behind them. She turned to Steve, delivering a remote, warning smile. "This way."

With a flurry of paper shuffling and pen finding, Susan seated herself behind the desk in the den. To her chagrin, Steve ignored the chairs and perched on the edge of the desk. He folded his arms across his chest. Susan had the frustrated feeling he was struggling with laughter. Pointedly, she ignored the powerful wedge of his shoulders and the way the jeans molded his thighs, hinting at the muscled calves beneath. Who would have thought anyone could look so good in old clothes? "Where shall we start?" she asked coolly. She wouldn't think about how mesmerizing he could be.

"You're the journalist." He shrugged. "You tell me."

Susan flipped on the typewriter, grateful for the hum of the machine. It would overpower the pounding of her heart. She hoped her nervous fingers wouldn't slip right off the keys. Damn it, she was acting like a lovesick teen! But Steve made her feel like Juliet to his Romeo, though in this case, a very deprived Juliet.

Something caught in her throat, making it difficult to talk. "I suggest you concentrate on what credentials you have for the position." Keeping her eyes on the paper rolled into the machine, she typed as if the devil himself were driving her. "We'll list your experience as a law-enforcement official on every poster. Tell people countywide that you have an associate degree in law enforcement from a community college, that you spent six years in the marines as a military policeman and another two years in New York City, working as a street cop before moving to Grafton and accepting a job here. You have four years total service with our community police force, two years as sheriff and several local and statewide awards and commendations to boot."

He circled around her and stood behind her chair. Though he was careful not to hover, she was still undeniably aware of everything about him—his height, his strength, his brisk male scent. Glancing over what she had done, he was very impressed. Susan had typed his work history accurately, down to the last detail. "You don't need me at all, do you?" he said softly, wonderingly.

His hands on the back of her chair, he swiveled her around to face him. Susan looked up into the rugged lines of his face. She could hear the typewriter humming behind her. It seemed to echo the racing of her pulse.

Yes, I do need you, she thought, *but in ways that go far beyond the physical.* She wouldn't accept a physical substitute for love, pleasurable as it would no doubt be. She needed understanding, and encouragement careerwise, neither of which he had been able to offer her when she'd been under fire personally. Whipping her chair back around, she switched off her machine and took up a pencil and paper. "We need some personal quotes for the back of the brochure. A sentence or two that will communicate briefly why you want the job, why you stay in West Virginia."

He moved back around to the front of the desk. He took a seat in an easy chair next to the door. Though there was only a distance of perhaps eight feet separating them, Susan felt as if they were miles away from one another emotionally. He seemed to share her feeling of aloneness and isolation.

He thought for several minutes. "In the city, criminals and victims are for the most part strangers. But I've adopted the life here in West Virginia, and in the past four years I've become acquainted with just about everyone in Taylor County. I not only understand but know by heart the history of most property-line or domestic disputes. I'm better able to make judgments on whether or not someone need be assigned community service or spend time in jail cooling off."

"How do the people here in Grafton know you won't decide to return to the city, at some point during your two-year term?"

"Grafton's my home now. Whether or not I'm elected, I intend to stay and work toward making it a better place to live."

Susan had half expected to have to rewrite or edit his comments. They needed no revision. Finished, she switched off her typewriter and asked a strictly personal question. She felt guilty for wishing in some respects he would lose reelection. "If Robert Wakefield won, would you continue working as a deputy?" If only she had some hope he would consider going with her when she left again!

"Either that or the Grafton police force." He seemed to read her mind. His frown deepened, but his voice was quiet, in direct contrast to the harsh, defiant expression on his face. "I'm not leaving, Susan. This is my home. It's also Eric's for another two years."

Disappointment flooded her. "I thought home was where the heart is," she quipped tossing aside her pen. Nothing had changed despite her wishful thinking.

"Maybe to those with wanderlust," he said sighing. He glanced at her, his eyes dark, but remote. "During my six years in the marines," he continued, "I guarded embassy posts all over the world. It was interesting work—I won't deny that—but I had enough of strangers and traveling. When I quit, I wanted a home again. I might have initially come to West Virginia on vacation, looking for a place to get away from it all. But when I got here, I saw so much more potential, not just in the beauty of the land but in the spirit of the people, the sense of family and community they've given me. I know that kinship will only get stronger. I never felt that growing up myself. Not the way it is here. So yes, I stay here because of that and will continue to stay because this is where I want to raise my own kids."

"You're planning to marry." Her throat ached unbearably. It hadn't occurred to her that Steve might have already found someone else. If so, why hadn't her mother mentioned it? Why hadn't he?

He nodded definitively. "Within the next two or three years. Absolutely, as soon as Eric's off to college. I won't lie to you. I used to hold out for the kind of love you see in the movies. I thought for a while that with you I found it." His mouth tightened. He rose, stretching, placing his hands on his waist. "I'm going to have my own family, Susan. I'm going to have kids now, while I'm still young enough to enjoy raising them."

Susan wanted children, too. If she thought she could have a child and Steve and a career simultaneously, as Patsy Winter did, she would go for the gold. But so far not even the satisfying career had proved possible. Apart from all the other complicated life goals. She stood, too, blindly straightening items on the desk. She didn't want Steve to see the depth of her interest. "You'd marry without love?"

The pulse in his neck seemed to be going at jack-hammer rate. "I'm going to marry someone who wants the same things I do."

"What about love?" she pressed.

He gave nothing away with his body language. He remained relaxed, his face bathed in shadow as Susan switched off the bright desk lamp.

Steve managed an uncaring shrug. He knew what he wanted—he had since the first time they'd met—but there were times in Susan's presence when he felt as unsure of himself as a fifteen-year-old kid. "Affection would be there." Romantic love was Susan and Susan alone. "Maybe in the long term friendship and commonality are more important, anyway." He didn't really believe what he was saying. If he did, he would have married someone, anyone, soon after they'd broken up.

Tears gathered in her eyes. She stood, snapping the vinyl cover on the Selectric. Abruptly, she wanted him out of her life and her parents' home. "I'll drive you back to your place," she said shortly. She held up the folder of information they'd just put together and waved it. The set of her mouth was grim and unhappy. "I'll get these to the printer next week. When they've made up the specs, I'll have them send it over to your administrative office in the courthouse for approval."

"Thanks for helping." Following her lead, his answer was impersonal.

Susan grabbed her handbag and her keys. It had been a mistake to ever let herself hope they could be anything but adversaries. She fumed inwardly. He had hurt her before. He would hurt her again. It was up to her to see he didn't; to do that, she would have to keep every defense in place. "You're welcome."

"Think you'll be able to find it from here?" His voice was low in the moonlit darkness, low and caressing. He knew he'd upset her with his talk of marriage. Seeing the intensity of her reaction, he was only half sorry. Maybe it wouldn't hurt Susan to realize the world did not revolve around her alone. They silently entered the car and began the drive.

Only Steve's disapproval of speeding kept her from racing through the country roads to his place. This time, though, the car was dark, not filled with dusky light perfect for observing. As if also needing time to collect his thoughts, Steve stared straight ahead, laconically issuing directions from time to time.

"I grew up here, remember." In a few minutes she stopped her Mazda short of the house at his command and switched off the car motor. With the dimming of her car lights, they were surrounded by darkness. "I might have known Eric would forget to turn on a porch light," Steve murmured.

Susan sat immobilized, her hands still gripping the steering wheel, wishing he would just get out of her car so she could leave. She regretted ever promising to drive him home. She was still stinging from the announcement that he planned to marry, regardless. She didn't want him to see how hurt and angry she was. But knowing it would be unnecessarily rude of her to drive off before he at least entered the house, she waited.

He didn't go toward the front door but circled around to her side. Her door was opened unceremoniously. "Coming in?" He draped an arm over the open frame. The hint of challenge in his voice was unmistakable. Did he think she was afraid to be alone with him, she wondered. Either way, she'd show him who could be aloof and detached. Marry just for the sake of marrying anyone, like a stud searching out a brood mare, indeed!

"Why not?" Susan's voice was defiant, ice cold, as she swung her legs toward him. As her feet touched the ground, he offered her a hand up. She took it with queenly dignity, keeping her clasped hand unwelcoming.

"Can't see a damn thing now." Steve held her elbow as he guided her up the walk. "But Eric and I scraped, repaired and painted weekends most of the summer. The outside of the house is a slate blue; the door, trim and shutters are white. We put on a new darker gray-blue roof."

"It sounds lovely," Susan admitted grudgingly. As they neared the front porch, she could barely make out the walk that had been carefully laid. If she recalled correctly, Steve and Eric's home had been a mess before they'd owned it. Neglected for years, it would have taken little short of a miracle to make it livable again.

Steve slid his key into the lock, and the door swung open. Seconds later, both the exterior of the house and the entryway were ablaze with yellow light. Susan blinked, her eyes adjusting by degrees to the flood of light. Her next response was heartfelt, spontaneous. "Oh, Steve." Inside, the wood floors shone. He led the way forward. Wainscoting gleamed halfway up every wall. What little furniture there was had been selected judiciously. The overall look was country, but the thick oatmeal-hued sofa was contemporary, its cushions thick, new and inviting. Unlike the disarray of his old apartment, the house was impeccably maintained.

"Can I get you a cup of coffee? Some tea?"

Susan hesitated. It was a twenty-minute drive home on curving, unpopulated roads. She wasn't overly anxious to get started. More importantly, she felt unreasonable in her anger toward him. What business was it of hers if Steve planned to marry arbitrarily? No matter how many mistakes he made, it wasn't her business anymore to get involved or to judge.

"Hot tea would be nice."

He gestured to the sofa. "Sit down. I'll get it."

Susan chose the corner farthest from the door, glad for the moment alone. Steve returned, carrying a tray. The aroma of tea was very pleasant. Along with two cups and a saucer was a plate of Pepperidge Farm

Mint Milano cookies. Her face lit up with surprise and delight. "You remembered."

He deposited the tray on the coffee table and seated himself in an easy chair next to the sofa. "You got me hooked on those. I haven't stopped eating them yet."

She grinned. They abruptly fell silent. "I haven't eaten any in...well, since I was last home."

"Why not?" He poured her a cup of tea and handed her the sugar, remembering she liked hers sweet.

She shrugged self-consciously, admitting as she stirred in a spoon and a half of sugar, "I didn't have much time to shop in Lansing. I ate out most of the time, usually on the run."

"What about when you did go to the store?" He leaned against the back of the chair for a moment.

"I guess I had my mind on other things." Susan averted his steady gaze. "And then, too, I had to be very careful about my weight. It's true what they say; the camera does add ten pounds."

"I'm betting you could have stood an extra ten and still looked gorgeous."

"Thanks. But I doubt my station manager would have felt the same."

He leaned toward her persuasively, bracing his elbows on his knees. "I still think you should have indulged yourself. A life without some recreation is no life at all." He seemed abruptly eager to show her what fun her time off could be.

Susan guarded against the familiarity descending on them. She said nothing to either agree or disagree. When he handed her a cookie, she took it, sending him a tolerant glance. The chocolaty confection melted in her mouth. "Heavenly," she pronounced.

He nodded approvingly and drank his tea. The silence strung out. "I've missed you, Susan," he admitted softly.

She avoided his glance for a moment, then decided nothing could be gained from pretending she hadn't yearned to see him, too. Even if she had not said as much, he would've known she was lying. The distance between them, past and now, had been bad enough without adding deceit to it. "I missed you." Her words were factual, impersonal. She still wasn't looking at him but at the one painting—of the Blue Ridge mountains in springtime—on the wall.

"Is it too late for us?" He hadn't moved an inch. She sensed that much rode on her answer. She turned toward him, willing her face to remain impassive.

"Too late to love?" she echoed softly. "Never. But—"

"But our relationship wasn't right enough to think about picking up where we left off," he said, reading her mind.

"Not with us both wanting such different things. There'd be no point in going through all that hurt again, Steve." Yet her heart was racing.

He smoothed his palms over his knees. "I never would have asked you to quit your job. You know that." He paused, debating. "But now that you're temporarily unemployed—"

Susan was on her feet before she knew it, pacing, her hair flying about her face. She knew what he was about to say, and she didn't want to hear it. She didn't want to start hoping for the impossible. "Steve, I can't let my television career end in failure."

He disagreed, but his eyes never left her face. "Seems to me now is as good a time as any to take stock of your life and your career."

She knew what he meant: he meant now was the time to reexamine the reasons for their breakup. But one failure at a time was all that she could handle. Stubbornly, she stuck to a discussion of her work. "I feel like a nothing."

His expression softened compassionately. "You're not. Finishing your book will change your feelings."

Susan was unconvinced. "Maybe. Maybe not. But I can't promise you anything until I find out. Until I get used to winning at work again."

Frustration and anger lent a sharp edge to his voice. "Working in television isn't everything, Susan. It never was." Only she'd been too stubborn and starry-eyed to see that.

"Maybe not to you—" Her voice was sharp. Damn it, this was what she hadn't wanted to happen. She reached for her purse. He blocked her moves. She pushed past him, wincing as their shoulders pushed against one another, then moved apart. She didn't want this to turn into a wrestling match, with them fighting over things that could never be changed. "I've got to go." Susan kept her glance averted. He stalked after her, grasping her upper arms, and pulled her around to face him.

"Do you?" He asked without hesitation, his eyes blazing.

"Yes." Her own look mirrored his turbulent regard.

His grip loosened but did not relax entirely. At her warning glare, his touch slackened. "Susan, I want you to stay." Nine o'clock—it was still early. Eric wouldn't be home from his date for hours. They had the house to themselves.

"No."

"Why not?"

She remembered that low, gently coaxing tone of his all too well. Her heart instinctively speeded up. She felt warmer than she had in the year she'd been gone.

"You want to sleep with me," she whispered. She couldn't let it happen. She couldn't let him draw her into his spell. But already the silken threads of fantasy were spinning around them, adding to the aura of unreality in the cozy room. They experienced an intimacy both had assumed was long gone.

His gaze softened. The flat of his palms slid up her arms, over her shoulders. His thumbs slid inside the neckline of her blouse and stroked her collarbone. He wasn't denying anything. "I want to make love to you," he told her gently. "There's a difference."

Despite her ambivalence, she was losing herself in the ever-darkening smoke blue of his eyes. "Is there?" Her voice was an unsteady murmur. She fought for control, lifting her chin to a higher, haughtier angle. Reality intruded as sharply as the memory of his earlier wounding words. "What about your plans to marry someone—anyone—else soon, just for the sake of having a family?"

"It was said to make you angry and jealous, and you know it. And apparently it worked, but there's never been anyone but you, Susan," he said persuasively. His arm curved around her spine. He drew her nearer, using the slightest pressure. She trembled as her breasts met the hardness of his chest.

She wanted to believe that as much as she had wanted to believe that somehow he'd change his mind about what he needed and go with her the next time she left West Virginia. But the sound of his voice earlier came back to haunt her. She broke free of his velvet seductive grasp and pulled away from him. Face flaming, she strode across the room and stood facing away from him, not wanting him to see either the burning misery welling up in her eyes yet again that evening nor the physical need hidden just below the surface.

"Our making love won't solve anything." Her voice was sullen and angry. She didn't move as he came up behind her. He stood so close she could feel the heat emanating from his body, like a fire on a chilly autumn night.

Where Steve was concerned, she had so little defense, Susan thought. Despite everything, she did still love and desire him with all her heart. She'd known it the moment she set eyes on him again. In a choked whisper she continued, "Right now it's all mystery and passion between us. We both want what we were denied." She turned to face him. He didn't move back. There was but an inch between them. Already she could sense how easily her softer form would still melt into his hardness, how perfectly they would join. With difficulty, she forced herself to go on. "But eventually the newness would pass, and then we'd be right back where we started from, Steve. Only the hurt would be ten times as bad." And she couldn't bear it. Not again.

His hands closed over her shoulders. She was nudged forward until they were touching in one long, electrified line from breast to thigh. "I don't think so. Remembering what we had, experiencing it anew, could be the beginning to solving our problems." His lips traced her cheekbone, glided softly, evocatively, along the nape of her neck. "Making love again would only intensify the intimacy we've already established. And adding to that intimacy would help give us the strength and incentive to find a way to work out our problems. Susan, I want you back in my life." He gave her no chance to respond. His mouth descended to hers. His kiss was all fire and heat and glory. His embrace was meant to steal her breath away, and it did. Yet knowing their lives might never join, her insides clenched in pain, and she twisted her face away.

Reluctantly, he let her go, dropping his hands to rest lightly on her waist and waiting until she faced him again before he spoke. "I want to keep seeing you." He raised his hand to her face and rubbed his thumb gently over her cheek, tracing the delicate lines.

She wanted that, too. Why deny it? What good would it do? "I'm not staying here indefinitely," she warned.

He didn't blink at her firm pronouncement. Frustration flooded her. Why did she get the feeling he hadn't acknowledged the inevitability of her departure?

"For however long you're here, then," he bargained soothingly.

His acceptance of her nonresponse was almost too quick. She felt she was falling into a trap of silken words and velvet caresses, a trap she might regret for the rest of her life. "I'll have to think about it."

Again, he accepted her decision with no protest. He walked her to her car and gave her another long, lingering kiss. "I'll wait to hear from you," he said softly. The need to have her was a throbbing beat deep inside him.

"I'm not making any promises," Susan warned shakily. As it was, she felt pressured enough by her own desires without adding his expectations into the bargain.

He grinned, realizing the victory in just her indecision. "A man can always hope." And at the moment there was no end to his own private dreams.

Chapter Five

"Looking for something?" An unidentified man Susan estimated to be in his mid- to late twenties faced her from the end of her front porch. It was early Wednesday afternoon. The days since Susan had seen or heard from Steve had passed more slowly than she had imagined possible. She'd half hoped Steve would call or pursue her again. But he hadn't. Meanwhile, she refused to let him dominate her thoughts. She turned her attention back to the intruder. The strange man, unaware of the wandering direction of Susan's thoughts, held up her copy of the *Taylor County Bugle*. As she took it, he introduced himself audaciously, and without charm. "You've probably heard of me. I'm Robert Wakefield."

Steve's opponent. Susan faced Robert warily. She didn't know what this was about, and she wasn't sure she wanted to know. "Hello, Mr. Wakefield." *And good-bye,* she thought, just that swiftly.

He hustled to join her on the porch before she could slip back into her house. Robert was tall and thin, with carefully combed hair and a light mustache. He was dressed impeccably in gray flannel slacks and a light-blue-and-gray-striped shirt. "I presume you know you're the cover story." He was carrying an expensive leather briefcase in his left hand.

Susan glanced at herself. As Patsy had promised, Susan graced page one. She looked at the photo of herself bending over to pick up the trash. Steve was clearly visible in the background, as was Gena Borden. The article was captioned "Taylor County Sheriff Steve Markham Drafts Celebrity Susan Trent into Community Service." Susan was quoted as saying coyly, "I'm learning the hard way not to jaywalk."

"If I were elected sheriff, that program would be abolished at once," Robert continued to goad Susan slyly. He flashed her a smile. "It must have been horrendous for you to have participated in such a program."

Susan forced a smile, ignoring the obvious effort at commiseration. "I think I got what I deserved." She only wished Robert would. No wonder everyone was so anxious to defeat him.

"Oh?" Propping one foot on the cement step leading to her door, Robert balanced the briefcase on his knee. He withdrew an elaborate pamphlet printed in red, white and blue. On the back was featured a color photo of himself and his wife and two children. Another photo of himself, also in color and apparently airbrushed, appeared on the cover. Below was a series of manufactured and meaningless quotes on law and justice. Susan knew a professional public relations snow job when she saw one. Her distrust of Robert grew. If he was so sure he was right for the job, she reasoned, why did he feel he needed hyped-up media exposure? Why was he pursuing Susan?

Susan stood straighter. She was surprised at the strength of her desire to defend Steve. In answer to Robert's question, she replied calmly, "I did something I knew was illegal. I paid for it. I can't say I'm happy it's in the paper, but those are the breaks. Now if you'll excuse me, I have work to do."

Robert ignored her polite attempt to excuse herself and looked past her toward the door of her apartment. "It's very important we speak. Please. May I come in?"

Susan had no intention of changing her mind. "I'm sorry. I'm working."

"I won't take much of your time," he bartered.

Wrong, Robert. You won't take any, Susan thought acerbically. But she responded politely, "I've already signed on to work for Steve Markham."

Robert made no effort to suppress either his disappointment or his contempt. "Because you were engaged to him?" The question was evenly put, but beneath the suave exterior Susan detected an undercurrent of unpleasantness.

"Because I believe he's a good sheriff."

There was a silence. Robert nodded perfunctorily. He must have realized there was no changing Susan's mind as he walked back down the steps a moment later, his shoulders hunched forward in defeat. "I can understand your position. But if you're ever in need of a friend or a favor..."

He left the sentence hanging. *Thanks but no thanks,* she thought. Susan was in the house, the door locked securely behind her, before Robert had made it to his car. *Corruption, thy name is Robert,* she thought.

AN HOUR LATER, Susan was on her way to see Steve. He was on the phone when she entered his office on the third floor of the weathered but imposing limestone courthouse. His secretary had already gone home for the day, and the outer reception area was empty. Steve was alone in his private office. Feet propped up on the corner of his desk, he was cradling the phone, talking quietly to someone at the mines, from what she could discern. Seeing Susan, he motioned for her to close the door and sit down. She chose a straight-backed chair next to the door and shrugged out of her vibrant red wool stadium coat. The fall weather was turning brisk, making coats and gloves a necessity.

"Trouble at the mines?" Susan asked curiously when he hung up. In the back of her mind was Patsy's request for news-breaking stories. Susan had yet to come up with a single one.

Steve leaned back in his chair and watched her through narrowed eyes glinting with half-hidden amusement. "Susan, you know that's not a fair question to ask—" he chided. His level look was even less accessible than his tone.

"No. But it's one that any journalist worth her salt would pose."

His brows raised questioningly. His sensual mouth formed a smile. "So, old news hounds never die, is that it?"

"Mmm-hmm." Susan returned his grin and his banter, feeling more alive than she had in days. Undaunted, she rose and strolled closer, seating herself on the edge of his desk. "So, what's happening at the mine? Is there a possible story there?"

For a second she thought he wouldn't answer. He picked up a pencil and turned it end over end. Finally, he admitted, "The past couple of years, business has been erratic. They've been forced to lay off or retire early quite a number of men. They're going to be hiring again soon. The manager is afraid there could be trouble when that time comes. Evidently they've set up a logical, fair system to rehire the workers in the order they were fired, but there will undoubtedly be protests no matter how they do it."

Susan nodded.

"I'm telling you this confidentially," Steve continued remonstratively, "Because we're friends. Nothing about the company's plans to rehire can be printed at this point. When it's time, the manager'll call Patsy at the *Bugle*, and probably the local television stations, too."

Susan understood and respected the need for confidentiality. That didn't mean she wouldn't be first with the scoop, if at all possible. "How long do you think it will be?" On the wall behind Steve was a state flag. With a white background and a blue border, the flag featured the coat of arms as well as the state motto, *Montani Semper Liberi*, or "Mountainmen Are Always Free." Though not a native West Virginian, there wasn't a man alive the motto applied to more than Steve. Maybe that was why he loved West Virginia so, she reflected. He felt so at home amid the rugged terrain and plain-speaking people.

Oblivious to the whimsical direction of her thoughts, Steve continued about the reopening of the mine. "Maybe as long as another month. At this point they're just not sure." He lifted his feet off the desk.

"So, to what do I owe the honor of your presence? Does this mean you've changed your mind about seeing me?" Damn, but she was beautiful, he thought, even more so after being out in the chill autumn wind. He liked the fact that she hadn't stopped to comb her hair but had styled it gently into place with her fingertips at the same moment she'd walked through his office door.

Too abruptly, he seemed to be thinking on the same wavelength as she. Susan stood, unsure whether or not she wanted him to know how lonely she had been since they'd parted. "I stopped by to see you because your opponent stopped by to see me." She turned toward her handbag, rustling through it until she found what she wanted, returning to his desk several seconds later with the brochure Robert had brought her. "Have you seen this?" She handed it to Steve. He was careful not to touch her, just the paper.

Steve glanced through the brochure. He said nothing, but his look grew more discouraged as he surveyed how slickly the item had been put together. She felt his disappointment. She knew how he felt; she'd felt much the same way. Gently, she continued, telling him both what she knew and had surmised. "They must have spent thousands of dollars on this campaign. Plus, they're putting up posters all over the place. I counted fifteen new signs for Wakefield on my way over."

Steve accepted her news grimly. "I know. They've been busy in the rural areas, too. I guess we're going to have to get busy."

"I called my mother. She and the others on the committee are already stepping up their efforts." She didn't want him to worry. She did want to know more about what and who exactly they were up against. Step one was figuring out the opponent. "What do you know about Robert?" Susan asked.

Steve gestured indifferently. "Not much. He hasn't been around Grafton much more than you have the past decade or so. What does the brochure say?"

Susan tucked a strand of hair behind her ear. "He graduated from college five years ago. Since then he's lived in Clarksburg and worked as an executive for his uncle's glass factory there. Why would Robert want to leave a job like that for politics, Steve?" Her tone was harsh and disbelieving.

Quelling his urge to pace the office, Steve placed his hands flat on his desk. He contemplated Susan solemnly. "The word is his uncle is the one pushing him to run for sheriff. The uncle is the one financing the campaign efforts and posters and so forth."

"Family loyalty?" she wondered aloud at the uncle's motivation.

Steve grimaced. "Either the uncle really believes in Robert or wants to get rid of him." He was used to being pressured at work. He thrived on action, days and nights that were short on sleep. But the pressure he felt being with Susan was a different kind of pressure, of wanting something that was always dangling just out of reach.

Susan sensed Robert's uncle wanted to get rid of him. On the surface, there was nothing really unpalatable about Robert. Yet there'd been a second, when he'd been discussing her community-service sentence, when she'd gotten the queasy feeling Robert could very easily be bribed. Susan reported her conversation with his opponent. Steve shrugged dismissively when she'd finished. "From what you've told me, Robert has done nothing illegal." Privately, he wanted to punch out Robert for showing up on Susan's doorstep.

Susan persisted confidently. "But Robert would, given half a chance. Maybe there's something in his past, something we could dig up," Susan continued.

Steve shook his head negatively, leaving his chair. He stalked to the window behind his desk restlessly. Never before had his office seemed so small and oppressive. It depressed him slightly to realize Susan had come not so much because she wanted to see him but because she wanted to alert him to possible trouble with his campaign. Given the choice, he would have preferred her to come to him via personal motivation. Could she stand to be without him any more than he could take being without her? "I told you I didn't want any mudslinging in this campaign." He looked out at the town, past the front of the courthouse, to the statue commemorating the battle of Philippi in 1861. The history of the town dated back to before the Civil War. Was he as much a relic in what he wanted for them, he wondered.

She rose from the desk and followed him to the window. As her face tilted beneath his, he could see the anxiety in her eyes. It was all he could do not to reach out and take her into his arms; the inappropriateness of such an action in his place of work be damned. With effort he remained where he was, one shoulder braced against the frame, his arms crossed snugly over his chest.

"Steve, he might win if we don't act as aggressively as he is."

Steve liked hearing her talk about the election as if it were her contest, too. He remained where he was. "We'll put up posters. I'll give speeches at all the local public-service clubs. But that's it, Susan. I'm running on my record." He straightened, moving his shoulder from the frame. "If people don't see that or recognize what I've done..."

Susan softened her tone compellingly. "At least let's look into Robert Wakefield's past more thoroughly."

Steve shook his head negatively. "No. What counts now is what Robert intends to do for the community. I'm not going to start going for the dirt out of panic."

"Who said anything about going for the dirt?" Susan queried lightly.

Steve was silent. "I know how tenacious you can be when you get your hooks into a story."

"Meaning?" A guilty flush heated her cheeks.

He shook his head evasively. "Robert Wakefield isn't likely to appreciate someone from the other side conducting an investigation slated for the paper. Just your inquiries could prompt him to act unethically." He sighed heavily. "Besides that, I've never sanctioned winning because of someone else's shortcomings. That's not the way I want to play this."

Susan shrugged, replying in a voice laced with conviction, "I think you're wrong. I think anyone running for public office ought to be scrutinized more thoroughly. A written comparison of the two candidates can clearly demonstrate their positions on the issues, their personal and work backgrounds. Quotes are even more revealing."

"Maybe. But you're hardly the person to write it objectively when it comes to Wakefield and me. Especially when you're active in my campaign. But there is something else we could do." His tone was calm.

His lack of contentiousness calmed her slightly. Maybe she was overreacting. "What?"

"The owners of the Lean Delight food factory, Harvey and Mary Lou Brucker, are giving a party in their home tomorrow night. I've been invited. We could both go."

"Do you think there's a chance the Bruckers will endorse you?"

"I don't know. I'm not sure they could influence their workers on how to vote, anyway. But it would give me a chance to get to know the Bruckers. That could make my job easier in the long run if any trouble does come up at their factory. Will you come with me?"

Susan nodded. If she didn't accept some social invitations, she reasoned carefully, her time in Grafton would drag on interminably. "I'd love to. How should I dress?"

Pleasure at her acceptance radiated from him. He didn't move away from her, and the heat of his body seemed to skim along her skin. "The invitation said black tie."

"In Grafton?" Shock permeated her voice. "To my recollection, that would be a first in the county."

Steve grinned. "Apparently the Bruckers are from the East Coast. They won't be in West Virginia much except to check on their latest factory from time to time. I think they want to impress us. At any rate, the town is buzzing. The invitations are considered pre-cious—all the local bigwigs will be there."

"Including Robert?" Susan would enjoy the chance to show Robert Wakefield just how thoroughly she supported his opponent.

"I presume so, and your folks will be there, too. Pick you up at seven-thirty?"

Susan smiled with anticipation. "I'll be ready."

Chapter Six

"Am I early, or are you late?" Steve drawled from the vantage point of Susan's front door.

Unable to think of much all day except their date, Susan was humiliated to find herself not nearly ready. In contrast, Steve was right on time. His gaze trailed over her lazily, taking in the hastily thrown on robe. To prevent a run in her stockings, she'd slipped on a pair of slippers. A rosy flush heated her cheeks. "I'm late. My zipper got stuck." She felt like an idiot as she explained, "I had to cut myself out of my jeans before I could take a shower and do my hair." Fortunately, that much had been accomplished.

"You're kidding." He removed both his hands from the door frame and sauntered into the apartment. Susan reached behind him to shut the door.

"I'm not kidding." Aware he was watching her intently, she laughingly continued her dramatic recitation with much waving of her arms and gesturing. "It was terrible. About an inch down from the top, the zipper got stuck. I couldn't move it either way no matter how much I tried. For a while there I thought

I was going to have to roll them up under my evening gown."

"That's when you decided to scissor your way out of them?" His voice was low.

Eyes glittering with mischievous amusement, she shrugged. "It was either that or scream." She led the way into her tiny kitchen, rescuing her jeans from the top of the trash can. "I'll show you what I mean." She held them out for him to notice the shredded area around the zipper. Steve smiled broadly, as if imagining Susan in that predicament. Susan sighed mournfully. "I really hate to throw these away, but after the way I slashed them up, they'd be impossible to fix. Not that the jeans were really worth anything even before the zipper went." She tossed the fabric down on the counter with an exasperated sigh. "As you can see, they were ancient."

Steve followed her back into the living room. "They looked comfortable, worn in all the right places."

"They were." Susan whirled to face him. She was standing at the door to her bedroom. Beyond, on top of the double bed, several beautiful formal dresses of various colors of the rainbow were draped haphazardly.

His eyes softened as he teased, "I'd offer to break in a new pair of jeans for you myself."

"Very funny."

His eyes riveted back to the collection of evening wear. "Gorgeous clothes," he commented, inclining his head in that direction. "What are you going to wear?" If Susan kept up her current pace, they would be late. Normally punctual, he found he didn't much care in this context.

"I don't know." Susan turned and casually led the way into her bedroom. She held up a conservative black dress, long sleeved and high necked. Steve shook his head. "Perfect for an evening when you need to be a saint," he decreed.

"Not tonight?" She was pleased with his assessment.

"Not tonight." He moved closer, as if taking pleasure in being asked to help with the selection. "How about this?" He pointed to a midnight-blue gown with a heart-shaped bodice and full skirt. "The taffeta?" Susan considered it thoughtfully. "I don't know. It's awfully low."

"For Grafton?" He correctly read her apprehension. She nodded. "But you have worn it before," he ascertained. Unbidden, a surge of jealousy tightened his gut. He told himself savagely he was overreacting again, that it was none of his business who had seen her wear what.

"Yes." Susan didn't want to dwell on the time they'd been apart. She moved ahead toward another dress, a glittery silver-spangled white jersey gown. Long-sleeved, simply cut, it was both simple and sophisticated. She held it up, away from her, for better viewing. "What do you think? It has a V-neck, but other than that—?" Susan hesitated again, biting into her lip.

"I prefer the taffeta." He gestured toward the more dramatic garment to her left. "But wear whatever you want."

Susan paused. Steve looked fabulous in the black tux with pleated white shirt front and simple black tie.

"Why don't I try it on and let you see what you think?"

His gaze narrowed, as if he'd finally zeroed in on her abnormal amount of apprehension and indecisiveness. Susan fought to keep her expression neutral. She hadn't meant to be that transparent. "You've never needed my help to decide on a dress before," he said, very low. "Why are you being so solicitous now?"

Susan felt warmth flood her cheeks. "I was thinking about the campaign." Damn, she felt like such a fool.

Steve's voice was soft, vaguely amused as he related, "Tonight is a social occasion only."

"People here will still judge you by the company you keep. And don't argue with me; you know it's true. The sins of the girlfriend or wife are visited upon the candidate, or least around here. It's called guilt by association."

His mouth quirked in a roguish smile. "Then it's a guilt I willingly accept. Besides, that being the case, one look at you and I ought to win by a landslide."

"Hah." She was blushing fiercely by now. Inwardly, she was very pleased.

He was silent. The moment lingered. As if realizing time was short, he said softly, "I'll wait out in the living room while you dress."

"Help yourself to something cold to drink," she offered.

At her suggestion, he paused just past the portal and held her gaze for a brief moment. "Can I get you anything?"

She shook her head and closed the bedroom door.

She was being ridiculous, Susan decided, shrugging out of her robe. So he was there with her in her apartment. So he'd been within inches of her bed. So what? Nothing was going to happen she didn't want to happen. Then again, maybe that was what worried her—the possibility she might change her mind about becoming involved with Steve if the evening proved too romantic or evocative of the past.

Susan went to the chest of drawers and removed a strapless bra. Soon she stepped into the dress, which was cinched at the waist. This time she had no problem with the zipper. Her shoulders were left artlessly bare. The ruffled bodice dipped low, exposing a fraction more of her breasts than she might have preferred. The dress was an eye-catcher, all right. She'd only worn it once before, for a charity ball.

Susan strode to the door. Steve was waiting, sitting on the sofa. He rose when she stepped into the room. His eyes lit up in surprise. He gave a low whistle that brought additional color to her face. "Gorgeous," he pronounced throatily.

She resisted the urge to cross her arms and hide herself from his gaze. Her curves graced the taffeta. "You don't think it's too low? Remember now, you're running for office."

He laughed, still viewing her with masculine appreciation. "Hell, yes, it's low, but I still want you to wear it." More seriously, he added, "You look lovely, Susan."

"You're sure?" Suddenly she wanted everything about that night to be perfect.

"Positive. I don't care what other people think, Susan. I'm definitely not going to let their opinions dictate what either you or I wear."

Reassured, she said softly, "I'll just get my shoes, and my purse..." She quickly stepped back toward her bedroom. She left the door open. Steve followed slowly, stopping just inside the doorjamb. He watched as she fastened sterling silver studs to her ears and a similarly fashioned silver braid choker around her neck.

"Now that's what I call perfect," he said as she bent slightly to see her reflection, fluffing her hair up and looking into her vanity mirror.

Susan turned toward him, meeting his eyes with unexpected self-consciousness. "Thanks," she murmured shyly.

Susan spritzed on perfume behind her ears and at her wrists. "Now my shoes." Susan went to the closet and pulled down several boxes, finally selecting a pair of shoes that were dyed to match her dress. She slipped on the spiky sandals, grabbed a matching purse and stuffed a small brush and lipstick into it. "Ready!" she pronounced in breathless triumph.

He didn't plan to kiss her. But as he watched her stride toward him, the long skirts swirling gently around her long, supple legs, his good intentions scattered like leaves swept up in an autumn wind.

He caught her around the waist, inhaling her scent, experiencing all at once her softness and femininity. More intriguing still was that she genuinely seemed unaware of how very beautiful she was. "I meant what I said. You are gorgeous tonight," he murmured, burying his lips momentarily in the silky thickness of her hair. His mouth hovered over hers, touching hers lightly, once, twice. He could feel her heart beating rapidly, hear the frantic cadence of her breath. They both knew from past experience that it wouldn't take much before getting into bed. But Steve felt if he strayed too far from the easy pace he had outlined for them, they might not make it to the party at all. Knowing it was hardly the time for pressure, he resisted the urge to continue his kisses. It was important that she trust him again. For the long run, it was imperative they go slow. And he was willing to wait it out with Susan; he was more sure of that than ever.

"We'd better go." She tilted her face up to his. Her lips were parted. Her breathing was unsteady.

"Do you have a wrap?"

She nodded. "Just a minute and I'll get it."

Seconds later, she'd thrown a white mink coat around her shoulders.

"You look like you belong in fur," he said softly.

"It was part of my wardrobe at the station in Chicago. So were most of the dresses and suits you saw in my bedroom closet."

"They let you keep the clothes?"

"No, everything had to be returned to the department store that supplied our wardrobes. But because the clothes couldn't be sold once they were worn, we were allowed to purchase anything we liked or wanted to keep at cost. So, I took advantage of the opportunity to broaden my wardrobe. I bought the coat last winter," she replied, lifting the curtain of her hair from the collar. "Partly to keep warm when I had to go out in the evenings and partly because it was a symbol of all I hoped to achieve.'' It had also been salve to her ego after she and Steve had broken up, Susan remembered.

Steve walked her to the door. ''Did you wear it often?'' The question was casual, but there was a low note of jealousy in his voice.

''No, not very,'' Susan admitted. As they walked outside, she continued lightly, ''But there were a few occasions it came in handy.'' Steve took her elbow, guiding her down the steps. Warming to his possessive touch, Susan continued, ''The station was financed by some wealthy investors, most of whom lived in Lansing and the surrounding area. Every so often several of us from the station would be invited to make a command appearance at some event. The affairs were almost always formal, and very boring. Usually, I'd find myself paired off with some widower forty years my senior or a middle-aged stockbroker or attorney with as little interest in me as I had in him.

''So you wore the coat then,'' he ascertained.

Susan nodded. ''As well as a few times on the air.'' At his curious look, she explained further. ''Because we were so understaffed, if WJCG covered any sort of celebrity ball, like a charity fund-raiser, they'd send out a skeleton crew and arrange to do something live. If the event was formal, in order to blend in properly, the reporter also had to be in formal dress. And our boss was particularly fond of getting shots of people going in and out of posh hotels. Less noise than in the ballroom itself, more glitz, especially if there were lots of limos pulling up to the front of a hotel or Lansing estate. I did a lot of those, worked a lot of weekends. There are a lot of automobile-company executives that have homes in the area, and of course, since Lansing's the state capital, there were a fair number of political functions that had to be covered.'' Susan stopped at the end of the walk. Moonlight silvered Steve's face. ''We were under a lot of pressure most of the time, because my boss was determined to up the ratings. Our weekend ratings were particularly low. He wanted glitz. On Saturday evenings there usually wasn't much news except society stuff and the usual accident reports. So I did a lot of standing out in the cold.''

''Did you mind working weekends?'' Steve asked. His expression was inscrutable.

Susan shook her head negatively, not ashamed to admit the truth. ''No,'' she said softly. ''I had no one else to see, nothing important to do.'' *Except miss you*.

Susan paused before his jeep. She looked back at her shiny red Mazda. Though both were impeccably clean, the sports car would be the most compatible with formal attire. ''Would you mind if we took my RX-7?'' she asked Steve. In the past they had switched cars often, taking his jeep when need be, her sports car when four-wheel drive was not necessary.

''Not at all.''

''You drive.'' Susan tossed him the keys. He caught them easily. The action was reminiscent of other evenings in the past. Although they exchanged smiles, both were silent as Steve helped her into the car and gallantly closed the door for her after she arranged her skirts.

"What was the best assignment you had while working for WJCG?"

Susan paused. "Last winter I covered the governor's birthday celebration at the mansion. There were a lot of celebrities there, interesting people from all walks of life. We were invited to stay after the filming even though, of the skeleton crew sent, I was the only one in formal attire. I talked to a lot of people—a retired football star, a Kalamazoo housewife who's been honored for her work on behalf of the state's disabled children."

"What was the worst?" Steve slanted her a glance.

Susan laughed, then stretched, her skirts rustling softly with the movement. "The worst was during the blizzard last February. Our station manager was very big on action shots and action news. He didn't want just weather reports broadcast from the interior of the TV station where it was cozy and warm and far removed from what the viewers might have been suffering had they been out in the elements. He wanted on-the-spot reporting of the condition of the city streets. The weatherman got to stand north of the city on an overpass that had been closed because of ice. I got to go south of the downtown area and report on how to drive on ice, when and how to use chains on a car, things like that."

"Did you wear your mink?" Steve asked.

"You bet. Beneath that, though, I was a sight. I had on heavy insulated hiking boots, a couple pairs of socks, full-length thermal underwear, a heavy white wool sweater and the wildest pair of hot-pink-and-violet-striped ski pants you've ever seen, and I still froze my fanny off!''

They both laughed. "I take it the rest of your attire wasn't visible to the viewers." Steve reached over to clasp her hand briefly before returning his right hand to the wheel.

"No. The crew managed to get me from just the waist up, with the wind whipping my hair around and blowing snow into my eyes." Susan shivered. "The station manager loved the edited version." She stifled a low laugh. "Though if he'd ever seen what I was actually wearing..."

"How's the work on your book going?"

"Very well, actually." Susan sighed softly, leaning back in her seat. Her eyes shut briefly. "That's another reason I'm late. I got so caught up in what I was doing, I lost track of the time." Concentrating fully on her work was the only way she could forget her conflict with Steve.

He watched the countryside, switching on his turn signal when he saw the entrance to the Bruckers' private driveway up ahead. "How long do you think it will take?"

Susan shrugged. "In another three weeks I should be able to send the first draft off to my publisher. It depends on how much typing I want to do daily."

"That quickly?" The car slowed as they approached the tree-lined path to the house. She nodded distractedly, staring out into the darkness of the night. The Bruckers' red brick Georgian mansion was lit up like a Christmas tree. Cars were parked in neat precision up and down the driveway. "Yes. You know I've been working on the project part-time up till now. I didn't realize how close to being done I was until I got started on it full-time."

"If you had, would you have stayed on in Lansing?" he asked curiously.

Susan was still preoccupied. "I don't know," she said finally. There was a royal battle going on inside her, pulling her toward Steve, then demanding in the next instant she keep her distance. "I needed to come home for so many reasons." The least of which, she knew, was to figure out if she would ever be able to get over Steve completely, to think of him without feeling the aching well of sadness, loss, yearning.

"Such as?" Steve parked a distance away from the lighted front of the house. When he switched off the motor, the car interior was plunged into silence.

Susan met his gaze, speaking quietly. "I grew up knowing an extraordinary amount was expected of me, partly because I was the school superintendent's daughter and it was assumed and partly because I was capable of excelling. To do less would have been an injustice to myself. I graduated at the top of my high-school class, did well in college, did well at my job at the paper. The television job was my first real failure." She paused retrospectively, remembering. "It hurt a lot to lose that position, more maybe than I want to admit even to myself."

His frustration at not being able to aid or protect her showed in his tone of voice. "Then why go back to television work?" He turned toward her, his left shoulder pressing up against the windowpane. His right arm extended out, across the top of her seat.

Susan swiveled around until she was facing him, her head tipped back against the cool glass behind her. Though he was not touching her, she was very aware of him. Too aware. "To prove it was the job and not me. I need to excel again." Her voice trembled with the passionate depth of her confession.

He resisted the effort to pull her into his arms and offer her comfort physically. She didn't want love, he reasoned coolly. She wanted professional success. "I don't agree that the circumstances caused you to be a 'failure,' but why did you come home if that was how you felt?" He tried but could not completely eradicate his resentment.

She moved away from him emotionally again, seeming to curl up inside herself, where it was safe. "To give my pride time to heal. To be closer to my folks. They've always been there for me. Lately, I seem to need them more than ever."

Steve's expression, though steadfastly genial, became more remote. "We'd better go in," he said, getting out of the car and approaching her. Casually, he nodded toward the massive two-story home. "Looks like the party is already in full swing."

Susan nodded. The lights from the mansion were welcoming and festive. "I'm sure this gala will be remembered. It's practically unheard of for anyone to have a black-tie party in Taylor County."

"High-school proms are formal," Steve pointed out quietly.

"So are weddings, for the people in the wedding party. But that's about it."

"Do you regret living out of the fast lane, not having more occasions to dress up?"

"I don't know. I never really thought about it. To me, Grafton seems a nice place to retire."

"But that's about it," he ascertained grimly, accurately reading her thoughts.

She stopped walking and turned to face him. Earnestly, she said, "There's so much in this country to see and do outside of West Virginia. I don't want to limit myself by always living in one place."

He grinned. "I can see you being happy in the big city," he said softly.

"But you wouldn't be."

"I've lived there. I worked narcotics in New York City after serving my time in the service. No, I don't want to go back."

"You wouldn't necessarily have to work in narcotics again. That's the great thing about being in the city. There are so many options. It's not like it is here."

"I've chosen law enforcement as a lifetime career, Susan. Whether I worked narcotics or not, street patrol or vice, or even took a desk job or worked as a detective, the outcome would still be the same. I'd be dealing with strangers ninety-eight percent of the time. Some cops thrive on that kind of excitement, but I don't. I like knowing who I'm dealing with. I like knowing about their families, their history. I think it makes me a better cop."

Susan shivered at the finality of his tone.

"Come on," Steve said gently. "We've been standing out here for too long. We ought to be inside where it's warm." Together they started in the direction of the house again. His steps were brisk and purposeful. Though he was still lightly clasping her elbow, his touch was no longer urgent. All at once he seemed very remote.

I've lost him, Susan thought, depression crowding her thoughts. *My need for excitement alienates him.* It was a facet of her character she knew she would be unable to change even if she tried. More debilitating still was the knowledge that she didn't want to change her goals, not even for him. And that turned him off, too.

They reached the house in silence. Steve faced her before ringing the bell. "Ready?" He looked composed, self-assured and very handsome.

Susan nodded and took a deep breath, putting on her most charming smile. For Steve's sake she would do her best to be charming. In West Virginia one was still judged by the company one kept. She wanted to make Steve proud of her, to be glad that he had asked her to accompany him to the party. And she might even be able to do some very subtle campaigning on his behalf.

The Bruckers' Georgian home had been built in the finest southern tradition. Inside, it was as elegant a mansion as Susan had ever seen, outdoing even some of the Lansing homes she had visited. The entryway rose a full two stories and sported a curving majestic staircase as well as a crystal chandelier. An elegant butler took their coats. In the solarium, a five-piece country-and-western band played bluegrass favorites, old and new. Waiters circulated with trays of champagne and cold and hot hors d'oeuvres. A buffet brimming with food, crystal and heavy silver dominated the formal dining room. Susan was impressed but knew that many Grafton residents would be bowled over.

As they entered the salon, they were greeted by the manager of the Taylor County Coal Mine, the mayor and several members of the city council and the local school board. Steve and Susan chatted amiably with everyone.

The Bruckers had to be incredibly wealthy, she decided. True, land in West Virginia wasn't nearly as expensive as in New York or Chicago, but building costs for a new home that size were still prohibitive for all but the very rich. Susan turned to Steve when they were out of earshot, whispering, "Imagine, building something this magnificent for only an occasional residence."

"It almost seems a waste, doesn't it, to have such a lavish home and rarely use it, though I don't know why they'd ever want to go back to the city." Steve shrugged, unimpressed by the opulence.

Another difference between them, Susan thought, depressed. She preferred to commute to her job.

Seconds later, the Bruckers arrived to meet them. Mary Lou was a natural blonde, and roughly twenty-five years younger than her husband. Harvey Brucker was heavyset, and friendly. "Sheriff Markham. Ms Trent. We're glad you both could come."

In the background, Robert Wakefield circulated, obviously campaigning, his attractive wife staying close to his side. "We understand from your parents you're writing a survival handbook for singles," Mary Lou continued.

"Yes, I am." Susan smiled. She could feel the pitch coming.

"Then you really should tour our Lean Delight factory here in Grafton," Mary Lou continued. "Our product is marvelous, low-cal. They really deserve a good write-up in your book."

"I'll be glad to look at the calorie counts and list of ingredients." Susan said. "But my taste tests are set up independently, you understand. They've already been done some time ago in Michigan, at the university there. I used students as volunteers. I couldn't add your products to the list without entirely redoing the tests, and I'm afraid that's just not practical."

Mary Lou was quick to offer, "We could set up a taste test for you."

"I'm sorry. To be valid, my tests must be done in a controlled environment."

Mary Lou began to pout. Harvey looked disgruntled. "You mean there is no way you can include our products in your book?" Mary Lou pressed.

Susan shook her head. "No, not this time around."

Harvey and Mary Lou exchanged a glance. "Still, you should at least tour our factory. Many of the people you went to school with are now working for us. Gena Borden, for one. Frank Winter's sister works as a typist in the management secretarial pool."

Susan glanced at Steve. Though his expression was pleasant, she could tell he didn't care much either way what she did. Although tempted to bow out, she didn't want to be any more controversial than she'd been already. Like it or not, whatever she did would rub off on Steve's reputation. She had to keep remembering that. "That would be very nice," she relented finally.

"I'll phone you next week to set something up," Mary Lou promised. Smiling, they moved on to meet the next guests.

"Whew!" Susan said, wiping imaginary beads of perspiration from her brow. She grinned up at Steve. "I didn't think I was going to get out of that one alive."

"Why does it matter to you so much what they think?" Steve asked curiously. "Why do you care what anyone thinks?"

Susan glanced back over at Robert Wakefield. He was determinedly courting the mayor. "I want you to win this election."

His eyes darkened. "I would have thought you'd wish just the opposite."

"I want you to be happy," Susan said after a moment.

"Even if it means I stay on in Grafton for at least another two years."

Susan nodded. "Even that," she said softly. What she hadn't figured out was if there was any way in heaven they could be together again. Was it possible they'd eventually be able to pick up where they had left off, commute from place to place, loving one another whenever their careers would permit? The possibility wasn't an ideal situation. But it was better than giving Steve up, she had to admit.

Without warning, Steve lifted his hand in a casual wave. Before she could turn around to see whom he was addressing, he had inclined his head in the opposite direction from which she was facing. "Here come your folks."

Though Clayton looked wonderfully distinguished in his tuxedo, he kept pulling at his bow tie uncomfortably. Her mother was tastefully dressed in a long cranberry-red dress that she generally reserved for wear at Christmas and other special occasions. "Susan, you look lovely," Emma said.

"Thanks, Mom. So do you. Hi, Dad." Susan and her parents exchanged hugs. Steve shook her father's hand.

"It's nice to see both of you," her mother commented. To Steve, she asked pleasantly, "How's Eric?"

Steve grinned, perfectly at ease with her folks. "Smitten with a new girl. He finally got a date with Wendy, the redhead who was at your home a few weeks ago."

Emma Trent smiled broadly, ever the matchmaker. "I remember Wendy well from her kindergarten days."

"You taught her?" Steve wrapped an arm around Susan's waist, pulling her into his side.

Emma noticed the possessive gesture and her smile deepened. "Yes. It may or may not comfort you to know Wendy was stealing boys' hearts even then."

Steve tightened his grip on Susan's waist. "I don't think it matters what I think one way or the other," he confided. "Eric's feet haven't touched the ground since Wendy gave him the time of day." His voice lowered matter-of-factly. "I only hope it continues."

Emma sipped her champagne and stopped a roving waiter to take a canapé from a tray. "Never underestimate the power of the adolescent will. Now that you mention it, though, Eric hasn't been around nearly as much as he used to be. I've missed seeing him. Think the two of you Markhams might come to dinner soon? I could even invite his new girl," Emma suggested thoughtfully.

"I'm sure he'd like that," Steve said gratefully. "Just let me know when it's convenient."

"I will," Emma promised.

"What about me?" Susan protested, stunned that they could have ignored her. Emma knew full well how Susan disliked being excluded from anything.

Her mother lifted her shoulders impishly. "Of course you can come if you want."

"Thanks. I will." Susan stared at her mother with a mixture of bewilderment and stupefaction. Abruptly, she realized she'd fallen into a trap, letting her mother easily arrange to have her spend even more time with her former beau, in the pressure of a cozy family setting, no less.

"You're welcome. And we'll expect you." Grinning wryly, Emma looked from Steve to Susan and back to Steve again, her gaze dropping to the possessive hand Steve still had linked about Susan's waist, to the temptingly low décolletage of her dress. Susan knew what her mother was thinking. Susan looked up at Steve. "Hadn't we better circulate?" Maybe they could campaign simply by not pestering people about the election.

"Catch you later." Steve waved to her parents.

The evening passed swiftly. They saw more old friends and caught up on everyone's news. It was nice to feel so much a part of the community again, Susan reflected, even if she knew it was only a temporary sensation. When the two of them left just after midnight, Susan was almost sorry they had to leave.

They drove home in silence. Steve parked in front of her apartment, then walked her to the door. She paused, searching for the key. Wordlessly, he took it from her and unlocked her front door. It was an old habit of his, one that brought back a barrage of memories. Suddenly she was not at all willing to have the evening end. And yet there loomed the problem of what would come next if she did invite him in. Would they be able to control the tension between them, to talk and rediscover one another as allies? Susan had no answers. She only knew she wanted the moment in time to last a little while longer. "Would you like to come in?" she asked uncertainly, after a moment.

Steve hesitated. He looked away for a long moment. His hands were shoved into the pockets of his trousers. His face was gilded in the glow of the porch light. "I'm not sure it's a good idea, Susan," he said.

When he pivoted back toward her, his steady look held her motionless. With unexpected bluntness, he gently delineated the conditions under which he would stay. "I haven't changed my mind about what I said the other night. I still want to make love to you, Susan. Don't invite me in unless it's what you want, too.

Otherwise, I think I'd better go home for both our sakes.''

He had told her what he was feeling, simply, honestly. Her heart was pounding as she replied with tenderness, ''I want that, too, Steve—eventually, if we can work everything out. But I need to make sure there's a future for us together first before we—before we complicate our relationship.''

Cautiously, he admitted, ''I was afraid you'd say that.''

His candor relaxed the tension between them. Susan smiled, never appreciating him more than she had at that moment. ''We've got time,'' she whispered.

''If ever there was a woman worth waiting for, it's you.'' He pressed a soft kiss against her temple. His arms wrapped around her. He drew her against him for a long, loving moment. His warmth was sweetest when compared to the chill of the night around them. ''Good night, Susan,'' he said softly, devotedly, then turned and retreated, leaving her alone in the dark.

Minutes later, Steve's mind was still filled with images of her. Whether in paint-splattered jeans or a soft mink coat and low-cut taffeta evening gown, she was all woman, and he wanted her completely, body and soul. But it was too soon for that. She was still fighting him, herself and the prospect of staying in West Virginia. Yet the idea of returning home forever was there, too, now, along with the knowledge that there was a chance they'd be together again. It was in her eyes when she looked at him, when she watched him surreptitiously from a distance. Maybe he was being foolish, but he still believed they could have a future together. Now, if only he could convince her of that, too.

Chapter Seven

"Hi. I was hoping you'd be home." Eric stood cradling a stack of textbooks and spiral notebooks in his hand. He'd obviously come over straight after school. Late afternoon, after spending a day working on her book, Susan was exhausted and ready for a break. Eric smiled as she stepped out onto the front porch next to him. "Got a few minutes to talk?" His reticence to impose on her was endearing.

Susan breathed in the invigorating autumn air. Her back and shoulders were aching from long hours spent bent over the typewriter. "Sure." Susan draped an arm over his shoulder and led him toward her front door. "For you, anything. Still like chocolate chip cookies?"

"Are you kidding? Some things never change. Don't tell me you baked some!"

"Late last night." After her evening with Steve she hadn't been able to sleep. Busying herself in the kitchen had helped only slightly to divert and tire her. Susan followed Eric into her kitchen. Minutes later, she had Eric in front of a plate of cookies and a tall glass of milk. Wary of her weight, after her own comfort-seeking postmidnight binge of milk and cookies, she contented herself with a cup of hot tea. "So what's up?"

"Girl problems," Eric admitted with a beleaguered sigh. "I thought maybe you could help."

Susan rolled her eyes heavenward. She felt like anything but an expert in matters of the heart. Elbows on the table, she rested her chin on her fists. "Dear Abby, I'm not, but I'll give it a shot. What's the problem?"

"I told you about my date with Wendy. I've been seeing her a lot the past week at school. She seems to like me okay, but when I asked her for another date, she said no."

"Did you have a fight?"

"No. But, uh...well, there is this guy that's been kind of hanging around her. His dad's real rich. I think maybe Wendy's got a crush on him."

"And is using you to make the other guy jealous?" Alarm bells sounded in Susan's head.

Eric looked furious. "Yeah." He finished off another cookie and took a swallow of milk. He wiped his mouth with the back of his hand. "The thing is, I don't think he cares about Wendy. I think if she does go out with him, she'll get hurt."

Susan got up and returned to the table with a napkin and handed it to him. "Wendy has to make that decision for herself, Eric," Susan said gently, resuming her seat.

"I know. But I'm still hung up on her."

And she was still hung up on Steve, despite everything. "What do you think you should do?" Susan questioned carefully.

"I don't know. That's why I came to you."

Susan wanted to tell Eric to forget Wendy. If Wendy couldn't see Eric for the gem he was, then she wasn't worth the trouble. But guessing that advice would be ill received, she asked only, "What do you think Wendy sees in this other guy?"

"Fancy clothes. A car of his own. His father is an executive for one of the coal mines."

"Clothes don't make the man, Eric."

"I know, but—" He scowled. Finished with his cookies, he drained the last of his milk.

"But you want Wendy to like you."

Eric nodded, turning tortured eyes to Susan. Misery tempered his low voice. "I don't want her to be embarrassed to go out with me. I don't care much about clothes. But I've got some money saved. Do you think you might go into Clarksburg with me and help me pick out something decent to wear?"

Susan smiled. She couldn't turn Eric down when he needed her. "Sure." She wanted to tell him not to count on the clothes making all the difference but decided to wait until later. Some things were best learned firsthand. Hard as it was to watch Eric go through the steps of what was probably an ill-fated romance, she knew he had to be given the opportunity to make his own mistakes. He was nearly a man; he needed to be treated as such.

"Thanks, Susan." He stood and carried his dish to the kitchen sink. She watched as he thoughtfully rinsed out his glass.

"Do you need a ride home?" Susan asked. She knew if Eric had come to see her, he'd missed his bus.

Eric nodded. "Would you mind?"

"Not at all."

TRAFFIC IN TOWN was clogged up by the repaving of one of the city streets. By the time Susan got out to Steve's property, it was nearly five-thirty. "Do you want to come in? I don't know when Steve will be home, but..." Eric's voice trailed off hopefully. Unexpectedly, Eric seemed as determined to help reconcile Steve and Susan as Emma Trent was.

Susan shook her head and smiled. "Thanks for the invitation, but I've got a lot to do back at my apartment. Don't you have homework?"

"Yes. Lots of it." He drummed the stack of books in his hands.

"Then you had better get cracking. Say hello to your older brother for me."

"Will do. Thanks again, Susan."

"You're welcome. I'll see you Saturday."

Eric stood just inside the front door until her car reached the end of the driveway. Waving once, he turned around and slipped inside.

Susan made the drive back to her apartment in short order. Pausing only long enough to fix herself a cold drink, she returned to her typewriter and the manuscript she was working on.

Around eight-thirty, the doorbell rang. A glance through the window revealed Steve standing on her front porch. He looked vaguely worried. He was out of uniform, which meant the visit was probably personal. Heart pounding with anticipation, Susan opened the door. Cool night air rushed into her front hall. She hadn't realized until that instant just how much she wanted to see him again.

"Hi. I hope you don't mind my dropping by, but I wanted to talk to you about Eric." He stepped inside. "I understand you agreed to take him shopping?"

"Yes. He stopped by after school." Susan reached around Steve to shut the door.

Steve frowned and raked a hand through his hair. In the dampness, it was curling around his head, making him look more rumpled than usual, more human, more accessible. "I'm sorry if Eric put you on the spot or inconvenienced you by asking you to do that. I tried to explain that since we're no longer engaged— Well, it's just not right for him to be putting you out that way."

Susan understood Steve's motivation. He had always been defiantly independent. He'd wanted to take care of Eric himself. "Eric's not taking advantage of me." She led the way into the living room. She was disappointed Steve had come to see her for such an unromantic reason. Determined not to let him know the depth of her hurt, she said reassuringly, "I like helping him out."

"You're sure you don't mind?" His eyes searched her face. He was absolutely still.

"No. If I had felt inconvenienced, I wouldn't have offered to take him." She paused, studying him with a scrutiny that was equally intense. "Are you upset that he came to me?" She felt as if her entire being had been put under a microscope.

"No, I'm glad he comes to you for advice." Relief poured from him. Steve stepped toward her. His expression and tone both softened. "To be honest, Eric isn't the only reason I came over tonight. I wanted to see you again, too.'' As he spoke, he brushed away a tendril of her hair.

Susan's mouth and throat were unbearably dry. Awareness shimmered through her, as he turned her toward him. His fingertips curled around her shoulders.

Rather than resist his grasp, she leaned into it, as if drawing strength from his composure. Honestly, Susan admitted, ''I thought about us a lot last night after you left.''

Steve nodded. ''So did I.''

''When I came back, I thought it would be best for both of us if I kept my distance from you and didn't let myself get involved again.'' Susan's words sounded strained. ''I think I may have been wrong about that.'' What she was telling Steve was very hard for her to admit to him, but she had to express the misgivings that had kept her awake late into the night.

Steve nodded his understanding. He cast her a gentle look. ''I can't give you any guarantees that we won't end up hurting each other again even more if we do see each other. But I do know if we don't see each other, we'll always wonder if we couldn't have somehow managed to work it out. I don't want to spend the rest of my life wondering what might have been if only we'd talked more now. I want to see you while you're back. Not just occasionally but as often as possible, even if we fight.'' He perked up. ''And knowing the two of us, we probably will fight eventually.''

They'd had some scenes in the past, but for now the tension seeped out of her by degrees. She felt inexorably happy, close to tears. ''I want to see you, too.'' She spoke around the knot of emotion in her throat.

"Then it's settled? We're an item again." His hands dropped to his sides. Relief tempered his tone.

"We're an item. Do you want to stay awhile?"

He made a lukewarm gesture, then made a serious face. "Actually, I was hoping to talk you into going snipe hunting with me." As he spoke, his eyes narrowed dramatically, as if he were letting her in on the secret adventure of her life.

Relaxing, Susan grinned. "Very funny. I know there are no such things as snipes."

"Star gazing, then," he proposed without skipping a beat.

The idea appealed to her. Still, she knew Steve well enough to realize that such a teasing mood was dangerous when linked with him. No telling what he was up to. Obviously, whatever it was, he'd been planning it extensively. "Where?"

"Everywhere, anywhere. I'd just like to take a drive in the country. I've got a picnic basket in my Blazer. I thought we might have a minicookout, just the two of us. It's the perfect night to roast marshmallows and hot dogs over an open fire. I've got everything we need, including that sweet pickle relish you're so crazy about and the makings for s'mores."

"You really know how to tempt me. After a day spent slaving over a typewriter, what you've just described sounds like heaven. I suppose you've got hot coffee, too?"

"A whole thermos. Freshly made."

He was preying on her every weakness, making it impossible to resist. "Sure of yourself, weren't you?" She'd meant the words as a joke.

He shook his head slowly, saying only, "Where you're concerned, Susan, I'm not sure of anything except that I want to keep on seeing you."

She eyed him for a long moment, half in exasperation, half in wonder. "Just give me time to put on some warmer clothes and I'll be right with you."

As Susan dressed, excitement flared in her with increasing intensity. It's just a date, she repeated to herself. Like it or not, they were still emotionally involved; maybe they always had been. Accepting that fact was a risk, but she felt now that it was a chance worth taking. And Steve was right; if they didn't at least try, they would always wonder about what might have been.

By the time she joined him, her heart was thundering.

"Ready to go?" he asked, getting slowly to his feet.

She faced him in another pair of ancient jeans, an old flannel shirt and sweater and her red stadium coat. "As ready as I'll ever be."

He looked at the curve-hugging denim that fitted snugly over the top of her equally worn Frye boots. "I hope you're not going to have to cut yourself out of those," he remarked solemnly, making indirect comparison to the last pair of jeans she'd worn—and ruined.

"Not to worry. I've been miserly with my calories all day." She'd had to be after that nocturnal binge.

His brows rose reproachfully. "Not too miserly, I hope," he cautioned protectively.

"I'm a consumer advocate, Steve," she said officially. "I know all about nutrition." Which didn't mean she obeyed every principle. She didn't.

The front seat of his Blazer was devoid of its usual clutter of maps, spare shirts, jackets and gloves. It still smelled of his after-shave. She drank in the familiar aroma, feeling as if at last she was beginning to really come home again. "Been cleaning?" She nodded toward the orderly interior.

"Only in preparation for a big date."

"Where's Eric?"

"Home studying. He's got a big history exam tomorrow. Though when I left he was on the phone with Wendy."

"They're still talking?"

"Mmm. Nonstop, it seems. He's trying to talk her into another date. Another reason I had to come over and see you in person. I couldn't get use of that phone without prying it out of his hands. It was faster to make the trek to your apartment than argue with Eric about equal phone time." He grinned again, roguishly. "Not to mention how much more persuasive I can be in person."

Amen to that, Susan thought. She rested an elbow on the picnic basket that was between them. "What would you have done if I hadn't agreed to go with you?" She swiveled toward him. Her safety belt pulled slightly against her shoulder.

"You wouldn't have refused," he said quietly. "I wouldn't have let you."

A thrill went through her at the revelation that he cared. "So where are we going?" she asked when they'd bumped out of town.

His mouth quirked with suppressed laughter. In a mock serious tone, he answered, "The only place in Taylor County where no one else parks!"

"Why, Sheriff Markham, I'm ashamed of you!" she teased.

He sent her a glance that promised much more. "You haven't seen the picnic spot yet."

Minutes later, they arrived at Tygart Lake. Steve drove to a picnic area overlooking the lake. Using flashlights, they climbed out of the jeep. Susan watched as he built a fire in the brick grill. Together, they laid out several thick quilts and took up residence near the warmth and yellow glow of the fire.

"How and when did you find such a secluded, lovely spot?" Susan asked. It was a distance away from the main park road, and she hadn't been aware it existed.

"Just luck. When we broke up, I wasn't fit company for a while. Rather than take out my frustration and anger on Eric, I went out a lot. Sometimes to hunt or fish. Some nights just to watch the stars and think. The Fourth of July, Eric and I found this place and camped out here while we watched the fireworks. I've come back since, every now and again. In the back of my mind I always knew I wanted you to see the area at night, with the moonlight, the dark woods and the silence."

"It's beautiful here," Susan murmured contentedly. "So peaceful." She loved the ruggedness of the West Virginia terrain, the profusion of mountain laurel and wild honeysuckle in the spring. She had missed having unlimited access to the outdoors.

The evening passed comfortably. They both ate ravenously. Talk centered around old times and mutual friends. "Do you ever think life is going by tco fast to suit you?" she asked softly at last. Susan leaned back against him, warm in the circle of his arms. If only every moment they spent together could be that serene.

"All the time. And at other moments, like when you first moved to Lansing, I thought time would never pass." Steve smiled into the fragrant depths of her hair, enjoying her warmth, her softness. At first he hadn't liked her hair short. He'd preferred it layered and shoulder length. Now he couldn't imagine her wearing it any other way. "Do you miss Michigan?" He watched her lean forward and turn the marshmallow and stick she'd carefully propped over the fire.

She shook her head. "No. Michigan was just a place to work for me, beautiful as it was. I love West Virginia. I think in my heart this state will always be my home." She checked her marshmallow for doneness, then sandwiched it between a square of Hershey's chocolate and two graham crackers. They shared the dessert. "But I don't mind living in a larger city. The proximity to shopping is nice. There's always something to do."

In Grafton, there was a very limited selection of movies and bowling, and that was, except for the mining bars, about it unless one wanted to drive into a neighboring town. "Have you been bored living back here?" Steve asked.

Susan turned to face him. She licked a bit of marshmallow from the end of her finger. For the thousandth time that evening, he felt the stirrings of desire.

"Not bored." She paused, swallowing before she related quietly, honestly, "Lonely, maybe." Her eyes never wavered from his.

"I've been lonely, too, Susan. Far too lonely."

She took a deep bolstering breath. "Hold me?" Her whisper was pleading, filled with emotion. Her vulnerability surprised him. Opening his arms to her, he took her gladly into his embrace. Her face was buried in his shoulder. Steve's hand stroked her hair once, then again and again, each motion more soothing and caressing than the last.

Need welled up within her, dark and fierce. No one else had ever made her feel that way, safe and loved, with just a touch, a look or a quiet word. She inhaled and was suddenly aware of a love so strong and deep it hurt. Tears misted her eyes. Sorrow flooded her, regret for all they had lost. Like a dam bursting, the emotion she'd been holding in for so long poured out of her in a silent stream of tears down her face. A ragged breath passed through her lips. "And keep on holding me."

Steve couldn't see the tears. He could feel the change in the meter of her breath. "Hey," he said softly, moving back and away from her until he could see her face. His hand caught her chin. Rubbing his thumb across the moisture staining her cheeks, he said, "What's this?" Susan had always been better able to deal with anger than tears. To her, tears were weakness. And weakness was something she didn't permit in herself. Not Susan.

She shook her head helplessly, furiously, unable to say anything rational that would convey the depth of confusion and loss she felt. And in that moment he understood.

"I love you, Susan. I've never stopped." His hands tightened about her waist. He pulled her near.

Tears of gladness and wonder filled her eyes. She could no more have pulled away from him at that moment than she could have stopped breathing. "I love you, too." She held him tighter. Maybe they could take it one day at a time, she thought. And if there was no future, at least they'd have the present.

They were quiet on the drive home, both wrapped up in their thoughts. His hand clasped tightly over hers, Steve walked her to the door. "I'll call you," he said.

Susan returned his steady, loving look. "I'll be waiting."

Chapter Eight

"I can't believe it," Eric shouted, hanging up the phone just as Susan entered the Markham home Saturday morning. "Wendy agreed to go to the Homecoming Dance with me."

"Congratulations," Susan said, smiling. She traded affectionate looks with Steve. He closed the distance between them smoothly and wrapped his arm about her shoulders possessively. "When is the big night?" Susan was very aware of Steve's warmth and how naturally she seemed to curve against his body. She slid her arm around his waist, momentarily curving her fingers around the belt laced in his jeans. She'd never known anyone who could look so good in a simple white cotton oxford shirt and faded Levi's.

"Next Saturday night." Eric stood, and running his fingers through his own wildly curling hair, slipped into a denim jacket.

"Then we'd probably better get a new sport coat for you this morning, too," Steve decided. He pressed a light kiss into Susan's hair, then moved away decisively, picking up his checkbook and sliding it into his inner coat pocket. "You've just about outgrown the last one we bought."

"I'll say." Eric grinned as the three of them strolled out to the Blazer. He couldn't have looked happier.

The week had passed swiftly. Steve and Susan had seen one another every evening. On Wednesday they'd worked at campaign headquarters. On Thursday evening she'd accompanied him to a local Optimists' Club dinner. On Friday they'd attended the Grafton High School football game. It almost seemed to Susan as if she'd never left. The shopping trip with the three of them was adding to her sense of belonging. She was very glad Steve had suggested he not only come along but buy some clothes for Eric and himself, as well. She knew Eric appreciated his older brother's attention.

Once in the Clarksburg department store, Susan's concentration was focused solely on Steve's younger brother. "Eric, that jacket looks wonderful!" she said as he tried on a herringbone tweed.

"I like it, too," Steve agreed.

Eric frowned. Though he had very definite ideas about what he liked and didn't like in casual clothes, his opinion on the much more expensive dress clothing was uncertain. "Do you really think Wendy will like it?" Eric turned, better surveying himself in the three-tiered mirror. "You don't think it's too... conservative?" He glanced back at a rack of linen sport coats. Oversized and fashionably rumpled, they were a little too eclectic for Steve's taste and Eric's budget.

Diplomatically, Susan said, "I think the tweed is a safer choice, Eric. The jacket will wear well. You can dress it up or down." She showed him coordinating corduroy slacks and jeans, as well as dressier navy and cream wool slacks.

"I see what you mean." Eric smiled happily, checking the fit in the mirror once more. He glanced at his big brother for approval. The hesitancy in his eyes made Susan's heart ache. "What do you think, Steve?"

"I think Susan's right." Steve's eyes held hers, silently transmitting his thanks for her help. "The tweed is a practical choice."

Eric frowned again. "Wendy doesn't go in much for practical," he muttered beneath his breath.

Steve started to speak, then bit his lip. "The question is, Eric, do you like it?" Steve interjected. Susan knew what Steve was thinking but diplomatically didn't comment; Eric would probably be stuck with the jacket long after he'd be dating the same girl.

Eric examined his reflection in the mirror. "I think I do like it," he said contemplatively at last. "But I want to see what it looks like with the pants."

"The quickest way to encourage a teenage romance is to disapprove of the liaison," Susan murmured to Steve when Eric had gone back into the dressing room.

"Am I that obvious?" Steve sighed, standing close beside her. His voice was low, caressing.

"That obvious." Susan put a steadying hand on Steve's arm. She tilted her head back to better study his face. "Trust Eric. Give him time. He'll figure things out eventually."

Steve cast a wary look over his shoulder. Seeing Eric was still in the dressing room, he whispered, "I hope so. I don't want to see him hurt."

"You can't protect him forever."

"No, but I want to."

Eric returned from the dressing room. The three of them decided on a shirt and tie. As Steve paid for the purchases, Eric said, "Well, now that we've gotten that over with, how about a sandwich before we shop for your clothes?"

Steve laughed exasperatedly. "It's eleven-fifteen. We just had breakfast at eight-thirty."

"You know how it is," Eric returned. "I'm starved."

Steve glanced at Susan inquiringly. He was apparently willing to do whatever she wanted. "I'm not hungry."

"Neither am I," Steve said. He glanced at his watch, decreeing, "There's no reason you have to tag along while I try on clothes, Eric." Eric heaved a sigh of relief. Steve continued, "Let's meet at...say twelve-thirty, at the sandwich shop around the corner."

Eric tapped his forehead with his index finger, as if committing the instructions to memory. "Okay. I'll see you then. And thanks."

Steve smiled. "You're welcome."

As Eric sauntered off, Steve turned back to Susan. "Thank you for coming along this morning. I'm not sure I would have been able to talk him into the more conservative number."

"As my mother always says—" Susan's low laugh vibrated between them "—it's much easier to deal with someone else's teenager than your own."

"Of course." Steve clasped Susan's hand between his own. The linking of fingers had never seemed so intimate. "By the way, I meant to tell you Eric isn't the only one going to Homecoming. I was asked to chaperone the dance, and I accepted.'' Together they left the teen department and ventured unhurriedly into the men's department. Susan was enjoying the domestic activity almost as much as she was enjoying Steve's company. He walked over to a rack of jackets, and flipping through the double-breasted blue wool blazers, selected a forty-two long. Susan watched as he tried it on. The fit was wonderful; the color picked up the blue in Steve's eyes and flattered his light hair and faintly tanned complexion. He turned toward her and paused, buttoning the coat. His fingers smoothed over the front, molding the fabric to the sleekly tapering lines of his rib cage and trim waist before asking softly, ''Would you like to go with me, as my date?''

Her heart was pounding. ''Are chaperones allowed to have dates?'' Unexpectedly, her voice had dropped another pitch, intensifying the closeness between them.

''This one is.'' He grinned, adding more seriously. ''Yes. What do you say? The dance is over around midnight. You and I could grab a late dinner in Clarksburg. I know a restaurant that stays open until two-thirty weekends; they serve until they close.''

''Sounds wonderful.'' Since going out to the lake, all the activities they had shared had been purposefully unromantic. It was as if Steve were doing everything possible to prevent them from proceeding to intimacy too quickly. Although she appreciated his concern for her, she was also frustrated by the lack of physical contact. Regardless of the wisdom of such an action, she realized now she wanted him back in her life—in every way.

Steve glanced at his reflection in the mirror. He narrowed his eyes reflectively. "What do you think? Gray flannel pants?"

Susan nodded. With difficulty, she forced her mind back to the task at hand. "And a blue-and-white pin-striped shirt and red tie."

"You want me to look all-American, hmm?" His eyes locked with hers. This time he didn't move his gaze. His prolonged look stoked a slowly growing fire of desire.

She wanted him to be hers again. "All mine," she corrected softly, impulsively. Her body ached for his touch. He seemed not at all surprised by the revelation.

His hand lifted to her cheek. Caressingly, he touched her skin, tracing the line of her cheek, then her jaw. His thumb lovingly traced the upper curve of her lip. Her lips parted helplessly, and her breath stalled in her chest. "If I didn't have to work this afternoon..." He let the thought trail off. She knew he went on duty at two and was slated to be on call Sunday, as well.

Too soon, it was time to meet Eric again.

THE NEXT WEEK they saw each other steadily, spending every spare moment they had together, again working at campaign headquarters, making phone calls, sending out flyers. Steve kept his distance physically, but his love for her was reflected in his eyes every time he looked at her. By the night of the Homecoming Dance, Susan had no more doubt she wanted Steve back in her life full-time. All that remained was working out the details. With characteristic stubbornness, she refused to think it might not be possible.

At seven in the evening of the big dance, Steve arrived to pick her up. Susan wore a pink silk dress. A jacquard print, it sported a cowl neck and three-quarter sleeves. "You're ready!" Steve remarked in a surprised voice as he came through the door. He bent to give her a light kiss and reluctantly withdrew. Looking at her, he felt very positively about her as he laughingly snapped his fingers in feigned chagrin and teased, "I was hoping to be able to help you with a stuck zipper or something."

The prolonged sense of anticipation was almost unbearable. Yet she knew the waiting was for the best, for both of them. "This from a chaperone?" she questioned, a little too breathlessly.

"The dance doesn't start until eight. I won't act the part until I'm officially required to. However—" He heaved an exaggerated sigh. "Now that you've reminded me of my appointed duty, I guess I'll have to behave. At least for a while." He looked down at the small box in his hands. "For you," he said softly, watching as she unwrapped the pink and white carnations.

"The corsage is lovely." Her voice was unsteady. Each time she saw him, the pull was stronger. In semiformal clothes, he radiated a vitality that drew her, like a moth to a flame. Did he know how much she wanted him back in her life? How could he not?

"This corsage is what every well-dressed Homecoming Dance attendee will be wearing, or so the florist told me." His voice was tender, almost a murmur. "Matches your dress, too." Her pulse skittered as he moved even closer. The brisk scent of his after-shave clouded her mind with memories from past intimate moments.

"How'd you know what I was going to wear?" The flowers matched her dress perfectly.

"Your mother."

"Ah." Susan grinned with sudden understanding. "That's why she's been bugging me all week." Walking to the mirror, she fumbled with the long pin.

"Need some help?" His voice, deep and sensual, sent a white-hot wave of awareness tearing through her.

Before she could protest, he had slipped a hand expertly beneath the cowl neckline of her dress. Right hand holding the flowers in place, he pinned the corsage to her dress. Tugging lightly on the dress and corsage, he checked to make sure the flowers were securely fastened. "There. All done." His hand withdrew slowly from the collar of her dress. He gazed down at her, love bright in his eyes. "God, you're beautiful," he breathed. "If I'd had a girl like you in high school—"

"You'd have never joined the marines." She laughed shakily.

"True." His gaze continued to hold hers. She slipped away from him. Suppressing his own desire, Steve held out the dressy dove-gray cloth coat Susan had laid out. "Not mink tonight?"

"I felt it'd be out of place."

"You're probably right."

He said nothing more as they walked out the front door. "Your car or my jeep?" He paused before the two vehicles, parked back to front.

Susan grinned. "Your jeep." He shot her a quizzical glance. In a dress and heels, she had to know it wasn't the most graceful choice. Not that he minded a show of leg, especially Susan's legs. But he didn't want anyone else looking at what he still felt, inexplicably, unreasonably, was his alone to touch and admire. She teasingly explained her choice and the reason for it. "In a high-school parking lot—with all those 'student drivers'? We'll be a lot safer in that Blazer of yours."

"The consumer advocate lives," he announced jokingly.

"You bet."

The high-school gymnasium had been decorated with an "Over the Rainbow" theme. Cloth-covered tables had been arranged in supper-club fashion, a large center area cleared for purposes of dancing. Giant papier-mâché streamers hung from the ceiling. All party favors were done in vivid rainbow colors. Up on stage, a rock group from a nearby town played the latest hits.

Along with the other chaperones, Steve and Susan circulated freely among the students. "This really makes me feel my age," Susan said, sighing.

Steve leaned back against the wall, keeping an eagle eye out for trouble. "It shouldn't." He gave her a quick glance and a decidedly unchaperonelike smile.

Susan concentrated on the students. If she gave in to what his smile implied, she might as well hang it up as a chaperone entirely. "Eric looks like he's having a good time tonight." Wendy was dressed in pale yellow chiffon. Her corsage was identical to Susan's except for the colors which were yellow and white. "Pretty corsage, too," she observed with a grin.

"We picked them out together," Steve said.

"I figured as much." Susan's eyes met his again. Without warning, her heart was pounding. "Think we might get some punch?"

"Good idea." Steve took her elbow and led her to the refreshments table. He tasted the red mixture. "Still straight," he decreed.

"For how long?" Susan added. The talk in the restroom had been that it was due to be spiked. With the county sheriff present, it wouldn't exactly be appropriate. So far, however, she'd seen nothing amiss. Most of the kids there hadn't even been near the food table. She supposed they were more interested in other things. The girls probably didn't want to mess their lip gloss. The thought made her smile again.

"Wendy's been good for him," Steve offered. He elbowed Susan. They looked in the direction of his brother. Eric was staring down at Wendy as if entranced. Wendy was looking up at Eric with the same luminous glow. The two of them were so taken with one another that it was touching. Susan thought back. Had she ever been so trusting, so in love? The answer was yes, the first time and the second, with Steve.

"No longer worried about her intentions toward him?" Susan quizzed. To her, the affection between the two looked very genuine.

"Dating a girl that lovely has given Eric confidence in himself," Steve said.

"Therefore, you approve."

"For the moment, yes."

Their eyes collided. She felt as if she were caught in a gentle spring rain, getting drenched but not trying to make it to safety. "Pays to have a little faith, hmm?" she teased softly. "Not necessarily in the girls Eric takes out—how could you know much about most of them—but in his judgment."

Steve nodded agreeably. "Maybe if we'd had more faith in each other..." Steve let his voice trail off. His fingers tightened over hers. The band had begun a slow song, one of few during the evening. The urge to hold her in his arms was strong. Softly, he questioned, "Want to dance?" His eyes held hers.

She cast a wary look at the floor and at the other chaperones, most of whom were married and a decade older than she and Steve. Not one of the other adult couples was succumbing to the sweetly lulling sounds of the music. "Is it allowed?"

Steve shrugged uncaringly. "I don't think we'll be missed."

They moved out onto the dance floor. His right hand loosely circled her waist, and his left hand clasped her waist as they dreamily circled the floor. Near the end of the song, Steve gave in to the passion simmering within him at her nearness and rested his chin against her temple. He could feel her pulse beat speeding up as she relaxed, by degrees, into his embrace. The past ten days had been hell for him. Keeping a distance from Susan went against everything he wanted for them. Yet he'd known it was a necessary move on his part. He wasn't sorry. Because of their abstinence, they had regained trust in one another and had nothing impulsive to regret.

Steve glanced up just in time to see several kids, his brother and Wendy among them, slip out the side door. He swore between gritted teeth. Susan glanced up. He passed on the opportunity to explain to her. He didn't want her going with him any more than he wanted to lose potentially precious time. "I'll be right back." He extricated himself from Susan, leaving her standing on the dance floor alone. When he returned several minutes later, Susan was conversing with the mayor's wife.

"What was that all about?" she asked as she rejoined him.

Steve guided her away from the others. There was no reason to spread the information. "One of the seniors had a flask of Jim Beam in his truck. He intended to spike the punch."

Susan had noticed Eric preceding Steve in the gym door. "Was Eric involved?" She held her breath while she waited for the answer.

Steve shook his head. "No. When I arrived, he and Wendy both were trying to convince the others not to do it."

In retrospect, Susan wasn't really surprised Wendy and Eric had acted conservatively. "What happened to the Jim Beam?"

Steve wasn't the least bit apologetic. "I took it into the men's room and flushed the contents down the commode."

"Are you going to report them to the principal?"

"No. As far as I'm concerned, it's all over. If it should happen again, it would be a different story." He looked fierce, just contemplating the possibility.

Eric joined his brother. He was holding Wendy's hand firmly in his own. The girl looked apprehensive as she faced Steve. "I'm sorry about that," Eric related after greeting Susan.

"Don't be. You did the right thing," Steve said.

Wendy looked very pale. "It was my idea to go after them." She paused, biting her lip. "I used to date Frankie, the guy that had the flask." She looked down at the floor. "I...had an idea what he was going to do." She shot Steve a straightforward look. "I didn't want him to ruin it for the rest of the students. We were warned beforehand that any pranks like that would mean the cancellation of routine school dances for the rest of the year—and that included our proms."

"I'm glad you feel so strongly about keeping the dances both fun and safe for everyone, but next time come to me first," Steve said softly. The episode in the parking lot could have ended much differently than it had.

"We're going to grab a bite to eat after the dance," Eric said.

"So are we," Steve said. "Because this is a special night, your curfew is extended, but I want you home by two-thirty at the latest."

"Okay." Eric and Wendy moved off.

"So, you'll have to be in by then, too," Susan asserted. She tried not to show her disappointment.

Steve contradicted her. "No. Tonight I'm leaving Eric on his honor." The time to be with Susan had arrived. Nothing was going to stop him from being with her.

The rest of the evening passed uneventfully. Steve and Susan stayed to help lock up the school and then shared a delightfully romantic dinner for two in Clarksburg. It was nearly three in the morning by the time they arrived back at her place. They should have been exhausted. Susan felt as if she could go on forever. Her hand trembled slightly as she fitted her key into the lock. She couldn't blame her sudden lack of coordination on anything but nerves. It had been a nonalcoholic evening, for Steve had a policy of not drinking and driving. Which meant unless he had plans to stay the night somewhere, he never did drink. "Can I get you a cup of coffee?" Susan asked softly, noticing the late hour but not wanting him to leave, not just yet.

The door swung open. She removed her key from the lock and dropped it into her purse.

Steve followed her into the apartment. A single light had been left on in the kitchen, giving them just enough light to see. He shut and locked the door behind them. "Nothing to drink. What I want is much more...elusive." His hands slid around her waist. His breath was warm and inviting on the nape of her neck. Susan half turned to face him. He helped her out of her coat, and loosened the knot of his tie.

The choice was hers. She was as nervous as she had been the first time they'd made love. Stalling for time to recover her sense of self-possession, she reached for the light switch. His hand covered hers, delaying. He turned her toward him slightly. Her poise fell away. All that was left to them was exactly what they'd been avoiding—the intimacy that had been inescapable from the first. "No lights," he whispered. "We don't need them. We never did."

Her lower lip trembled slightly as his arms slid around her waist. "It's been so long," she whispered haltingly, feeling the zipper of her dress slide partway down her back. One hand glided beneath the silk of her dress as he deftly removed the long pin holding the corsage in place, placing the flowers carefully aside.

"Too long," he agreed. His look was darkly intent as his hands slid across the smooth skin of her back, holding her close. His whisper did erotic things to her nerves, weakened her knees, made her sway against him acquiescently. He pushed a curling hair from her cheek. "I've spent the past few days doing nothing but thinking of you. I remembered what it was like to have you stretched out beside me and beneath me. I remember the scent and the silky feeling of your skin." He pressed a kiss at her temple, the corner of her lashes. "I've burned with need for you." He drew back, searching her face. "But it's not just your body I want, Susan, but you're heart and soul and every single bit of love you have to give."

Susan began to speak. He pressed a finger to her lips, silencing her. His face was half hidden by shadows. The planes seemed sharper. "I tried to tell myself I wouldn't accept anything less than total commitment from you this time. I was wrong, Susan." His hands came up to caress her shoulders. "I want you any way I can have you, and if that means compromising, so be it. Just know that as long as you're here, my love is yours for the taking."

He had given her all she had ever asked for. "Steve, I do love you." Susan offered her lips to his. Her breath shuddered out as he accepted the gift, delving gently, then ever deeper. His kiss was sweet, seductive, mesmerizing in the increasing intensity. The apartment was cool. His hands, as they wantonly explored, were warm, first demanding, then seeking, then easing. "Don't stop," she whispered. His answering murmur was fierce, unconditional, as her dress fell to the floor in a pool around her feet.

"Never," he agreed. "Never again."

In a haze, she let him lead her to the bedroom. Her senses sharpened as they undressed in the moonlit darkness of the bedroom. Naked, they slid beneath the sheets. When she would have urged him on to swift fierce consummation, he delayed, leisurely setting the pace, drawing out each stroke, each kiss, until every movement was an act of lovemaking in itself. Eventually, neither of them could hold back anymore. She surged beneath him, exploding with a need so sharp and demanding it almost hurt. Her breathing quickened. His grew harsh. A night storm of emotion exploded all around them. Wildly, their lovemaking climaxed in a flood of passion as compelling and mysterious and dark as midnight mist. Susan had spent a lifetime searching for what only he could give. "I need you," she whispered as he moved within her yet again. She needed to love and be loved.

"And I need you," he whispered softly, kissing her, lovingly, tenderly, proceeding to show her how very much he did.

"SINCE YOU'VE BEEN BACK HOME, I haven't seen you totally relax once," Steve remarked the next afternoon as he and Susan gathered walnuts. "It's almost as if you feel you have to be busy every moment."

Together they canvassed the lane leading to his house. "I've just missed being in the country," Susan answered.

"And that's all?" His eyes pinned her with a shrewd stare.

"I don't want to think about the future," Susan confessed after a moment. Sometimes it hurt to be honest.

"What about us?" He barely seemed to breathe as he waited for her reply.

"It's too soon for promises." Susan averted her gaze momentarily. "We made decisions recklessly the last time, and that was disastrous. This time I want our love to work. We have to go slowly, confront and overcome one obstacle at a time. "Besides," she pointed out swiftly, before he could disagree, "you've been busy with your work, too."

"There's a difference," Steve said kindly. "I'm happy to be living here. You're not."

"You think I'm working overtime on my book and filling up the empty hours with projects so I won't have to think?"

"Aren't you?"

Susan sighed. She knew she could make it alone. But why should she when her life was enriched and broadened immeasurably by his presence? Still there were problems. Problems she was loath to explore. To do that meant to fight, and they'd fought enough in the past. Quietly, she admitted evasively, "Maybe you're right. It's hard being a woman now, Steve.

Everyone expects us all to be superwomen, pros at careers and personal lives.''

''So?'' He slowed his stride to keep pace easily with her smaller one.

She stopped where she was. Turning, she grasped his forearms. ''You know me. I always want to keep up with what everyone else is doing. I always want to compete. I want both a career and a satisfying personal life. But when it comes down to it really happening, I don't know if it is possible. Certainly I've never been able to accomplish both at the same time before.'' She met his gaze unreservedly.

''Patsy Winter is married. She has children; she works.''

''She also has two sets of in-laws right here in town to help out with the baby-sitting. And her work at the paper isn't going that well. They're running in the red.'' Susan's voice was both envious and mildly censuring.

''Meaning if she didn't have a family to contend with, the paper would be in the black?'' Scorn laced his voice.

''Maybe.'' Susan faced him defiantly. She felt she owed it to them both to be honest. She bit her lip in frustration. ''Look, all I know is that the women I've seen trying to have both career and family end up in some kind of bizarre juggling act if they're really trying to get ahead professionally.'' She raked a hand through her hair, feeling suddenly near tears, defeated. She admitted shakily, ''I'm not sure I'm ready to become mediocre at anything, never mind everything at once! Failing to get my television contract renewed was damage enough. My self-esteem is still at a low point. To be good for anyone, especially a husband or a child, I've got to first be comfortable with myself and what I've accomplished. Otherwise, I'm liable to transfer all my frustration to those I love most.''

He was silent. ''I understand what you're saying,'' he said finally. ''I agree it's tough to do both. I don't see it as impossible.'' They resumed walking at a quicker pace. Every now and again, they would stoop to gather walnuts. They made a soft plunking sound as at odd intervals they fell into the bottom of the paper bags.

''I'm not sure I could make you happy if I split myself up that way.'' Susan sighed, pausing for a moment to rest. Her back was against the base of a towering black walnut tree. Discussions like these were what she most wanted to avoid. Yet she had known in her heart they were inevitable if a future for them was ever truly to be obtained.

''Do you want a family?'' For that moment he didn't want to think of anything but the woman beside him, the quiet afternoon after the long night of loving. Too soon the coming week's work would intrude. For now, he thought, he only yearned to remember her as she was with her hair tousled, cheeks pink from the cold, her eyes sparkling with mischief one moment, dark with anxiety about the future the next, then soft and warm and glowing with love. There had never been a woman who would pierce his soul the way Susan did; there never would be. Whether she liked it or not, he would have to make her face the truth of that, then confront what had to be dealt with.

"Yes. Yes, I do." She took a deep breath and heaved an equally soft sigh.

"Eventually." He added the magic qualifier, and she nodded. Steve knew that it was an effort for her to be honest with him, that if she hadn't cared so very deeply about their joint future, she wouldn't have bothered; she would have sidestepped the issue altogether.

"I guess that's not surprising, since your mother works, too," he admitted eventually, sharing her sharp sense of frustration at too many needs, too little time. He wrapped his arm around her waist. "Look, Rome wasn't built in a day. Our problem won't be solved in a single day, either. The logical step is to continue to go slowly. With patience and time we'll be able to work out everything to both our satisfactions." He voice was firm, implacable.

"I hope so." Susan sighed. She closed her eyes dreamily for a moment, relaxing against him. "I'd like to have it all. A family, a satisfying job."

"Children?"

"Yes."

"How many?"

Susan opened her eyes at the teasing lilt in his voice. "I don't know. I don't have much experience there. One...maybe two, although I'm not sure I could do justice to more than one child, since I'd most likely continue to work after he or she was born."

"One child sounds fine to me," Steve agreed. He paused, confessing seriously. "I admire your folks, Susan, the example they've set. The three of you have always been so close. Your parents are interested in everything you do, but they've loved you enough to let you go, to encourage you to go out and try your wings, something I still have difficulty doing. Yet your mom has a life of her own, too. Emma's a good example of a woman who has managed to very effectively combine work and still make time for her family."

"I guess that must seem very different to you, since your family always had a more traditional arrangement when you were growing up. Was your mother happy being a homemaker exclusively?" Susan asked.

Steve nodded, staring out at the sunlit afternoon. There was a distinct odor of wood smoke and crushed autumn leaves lingering in the country air. "Yes. I know it sounds corny, but I never saw her less than perfectly content. If there was a flaw in the setup, it was that sometimes she seemed, to my way of thinking then, to be too devoted to my father. His needs always came first, no matter what else was going on. I've imagined myself in the same situation and found it lacking."

"Did your mother have any outside interests?" Susan asked.

"None, just things related to the three of us." He paused reflectively, tightening his grip on Susan's waist. "I wonder sometimes how she would have coped with both Eric and me grown up."

Susan grinned. "She probably would have hoped fervently for grandchildren."

"Probably."

He turned her toward him. Kindness and a need to understand permeated his tone. "You would never be happy staying at home, even if you had children."

"I think I'd always have to stay busy and probably, to be really content, work at something exclusively my own. I think it's healthier that way."

"Because of the example your own mother set?" Having gathered as many walnuts as they wanted, they started back toward his home.

"Because of the struggle I watched her go through. My mother didn't always work, Steve. Up until the time I was ten, she stayed home."

"What happened then?"

"My dad was hospitalized with a slipped disk. Mom worked as a typist to supplement our income and pay what costs the medical insurance wouldn't. She found she hated typing." Susan hesitated. "She liked getting out of the house. When my dad recovered, she said she wanted to go to college. Finances were tight. Looking back, I realize he wasn't quite sure she could cut it or compete as a student at the age of thirty-five. And I think it was that unvoiced skepticism of his that made her work even harder.

"Sounds rough," he said, thinking of Emma Trent's strength and determination.

"The first semester was awful," Susan stressed honestly, grateful to have another real-life example of feminine struggle to examine. "Dishes piled up in the sink. She still led the Girl Scout troop, but she quit doing any volunteer work. My dad and I were forced to help out. That's when I got interested in consumer advocacy. I wanted to know why brand X was better than brand Y. I did all sorts of weird experiments. And in taking over some of what had been my mother's duties, I began to understand why she was so anxious to get away from the house. Housework isn't any fun, but it's got to get done.''

''Did your dad ever come around while she was still in school?'' To Steve, Clayton had always seemed so enlightened. This side of the superintendent was new to Steve.

''Yes, at the end of the spring semester. He came home expecting chaos but found the house in perfect order, dinner in the oven and my mother sobbing her heart out as she weeded the dying begonias next to the back porch.'' Susan's eyes misted up as she remembered fondly. ''I don't recall my mother ever so upset or my dad more tender. He got on his hands and knees and hugged her. He kissed her and encouraged her to start studying for the exams she was sure she was going to fail. After that, life got easier. Dad and I helped out more. When she graduated from college with her degree in education, we were very proud.''

They were back at his house. At Susan's suggestion, they scattered the walnuts they'd gathered, still in protective outer shells, in a cardboard box to dry out. ''I thought I knew everything about you,'' Steve remarked as he washed the stain from his hands.

''We still have a long way to go,'' Susan cautioned. But once again she felt hopeful. At least they were talking honestly, comparing other people's problems and solutions with their own. It was a good feeling.

''If you're still here at Christmas, we can make walnut pies and cakes,'' Steve said, handing her a dish towel.

Would she still be there at Christmas? Originally, Susan had hoped to have another job in television by then. Now she wasn't sure what she wanted. Sidestepping what she feared was a point of contention, she teased, "There goes your waistline, sheriff." She flicked the dish towel at his belt and let her eyes move lazily over a frame that was all male and suddenly emanating both coiled strength and desire.

Grabbing one end of the towel, he pulled her to his side. Prying her fingers loose from the opposite end of the towel, he looped the fabric over her head, behind her waist. "I'll figure out some way to work off the extra calories." She was trapped against him, the band of fabric held firm against her middle.

Her laughter faded as his mouth descended to hers. With trembling fingers, she touched his forehead, his brows, the line of his cheek, his mobile mouth. His kiss was feather-soft, not possessing nearly the passion she yearned for, but it was provocative. She could tell by his steady sensual look all her needs would eventually be met, but in due time. She moaned softly, whispering his name once, then again and again.

He held her against him tightly, kissing her until all her senses were thoroughly aroused. He didn't release her, but a shadowed look crossed his face. His arms tightened around her waist, moving up her spine to hold her close. Regret sounded in his tone as he related, "I'm going to be gone all of next week at a law-enforcement conference in Charleston."

"I'll miss you," Susan confided.

He took her back into his arms for another lengthy kiss that soon had her tingling from head to toe. Throatily, he replied, "No more than I'll miss you." He traced the exposed arch of her throat with his lips.

"Hurry home?" She kneaded his shoulders, his spine, and let her hands drift low across his hips.

A low sigh of pleasure escaped from his throat as he began to knead her back. Torso to torso, they were aligned perfectly, their hearts beating at the same rapid pace. "Lady, you can stake your life on it...."

Chapter Nine

Mary Lou Brucker greeted Susan early Monday afternoon. "I'm so glad you could find the time to tour our food-processing center." On the outside, the rectangular concrete building looked huge and imposing. Mary Lou led the way authoritatively into the plant. "When I called you this morning, I wasn't sure I'd be able to talk you into coming."

Susan had been busy working on her book. Her mind had been filled with romantic thoughts of Steve. "Actually," Susan was able to say truthfully, "I was having trouble concentrating this morning." And she did want to do what she could to help him get elected. Privately, she equated touring the Bruckers' plant with kissing babies. All politicians and their spouses, or the equivalent, did it.

"Robert Wakefield and his wife were here the other day," Mary Lou continued genially. "They were very impressed! They left swearing by our product!"

Susan didn't know what emotion she was supposed to exhibit at that news. Jealousy? She kept implacably silent, asking finally, "Do you eat the Lean Delight dinners, Mary Lou?" As a veteran consumer reporter, she'd always noted the people who made use of their own products were often the most well-informed.

Mary Lou looked at Susan as if she had lost her mind. Recovering, she said carefully, "Harvey prefers his meals prepared from fresh ingredients. I try to oblige him most of the time."

They continued on, past steel doors, into the actual manufacturing area. Susan was distressed to note that the layout of the plant was inefficient and haphazard. Some workers—Gena Borden among them—were squeezed into very small areas. Others were given a wealth of floor space to roam. Ventilation was not as good as it should have been. The interior air had the mingled scents of everything from veal parmesan to sweet-and-sour chicken. Steam from the food-preparation section created a high level of humidity. Despite the fact that Susan had dressed lightly, her clothes were clinging to her uncomfortably.

Several violations bothered Susan. The floor was sticky and covered with a dirty film. Not all of the workers wore uniforms and hair nets. Aprons seemed to be optional attire. As they roamed the football-stadium-sized area, Susan and Mary Lou both saw someone sneaking a smoke.

"The dinners are packed in disposable microwave dishes," Mary Lou continued.

"I'm sure patrons appreciate the convenience of being able to prepare the dinners one of two ways, either in the microwave or the conventional oven." Susan forced a smile, feeling vaguely claustrophobic. As they left the noisy inner plant, she asked Mary Lou, "Have you been in the food business long?"

"No, this is our first venture." Mary Lou led her into a private office. Decorated as lavishly as her Georgian mansion, the office was in direct contrast to the manufacturing area. Mary Lou paused, flashing Susan an extrabright smile. "Harvey and I both hope you'll write about our products in your book." She held up a hand, stopping Susan's half-formed protest. "I know what you said the other night. All I'm asking is that you think about including our food products. In the meantime, if you'd like some free dinners to take home—" She reached for the telephone on her desk.

"No—" Susan's stomach rolled at the thought. She managed to be polite. "Thanks, anyway."

After leaving the plant, Susan went straight to Patsy Winter's office. She explained to Patsy what she had seen, finishing worriedly, "I'm sure that plant violates the current health code." She shuddered. "When I think of people actually eating that stuff..." Horror stories others had uncovered in similar ventures flooded her brain.

"What are you going to do?" Patsy asked. So far, Susan's revelation had been in strict confidence, from friend to friend.

Susan jammed her hands in her pockets and paced the office restlessly. "I don't know. With Steve's election coming up in less than three weeks, I don't want to jeopardize his chances for reelection. But at the same time I can't just stand by and let them continue serving up what might be contaminated food. No, I have to go the health department and report what I've seen. At least Steve won't have to be actively involved in the initial complaint, because he's in Charleston this week.''

''Are you going to call him and tell him what you're about to do?'' Patsy queried.

''Later tonight. I wish I'd never accepted the Bruckers' hospitality.''

''If it's any consolation, I'm sure they'll feel that way, too, by the end of the week.'' Patsy glanced at her watch. ''Unfortunately, reporting what you suspect is going to have to wait, as it's already after five. The state health department won't be open until tomorrow.''

''Can we afford to wait that long?'' Susan asked.

Patsy lifted her shoulders. ''Any food can be recalled in the morning, if indeed they are in as severe violation as you seem to think.''

''Patsy, I was there. I know they're operating that plant illegally.''

Patsy leaned forward as if hopelessly intrigued. She propped her elbows on her desk and rested her chin on her clasped hands. ''You want to write the story for me?'' Her gaze was steady. ''I need you to do it for me, Susan. A scoop like this could put the *Bugle* on the way to recovery. At the very least, let it go out with a bang, not a whimper.''

Susan continued pacing the office. ''If it were just me, I'd do it in an instant.''

''But you're worried about how your involvement in such a scandal would affect Steve's chances for re-election,'' Patsy reiterated.

''If they do close the plant down, the people who are subsequently unemployed are going to blame me. In their minds, Steve might be just as responsible for their loss of work as I am. Guilt by association. If I become publically involved in this mess, it could cost him a lot of votes."

"How or why people vote is hardly the issue here, Susan. We're talking about a major health-code violation. You became enmeshed in the scandal the moment you noticed the violations. You would be acting negligently if you didn't report the potential harm of the situation. If Steve were here, he would back you up one hundred percent."

"I don't have any choice in the matter, do I?"

"No, you don't. You have to follow through. To do anything less would be acting irresponsibly and unprofessionally."

"I agree I have to report the plant. But I don't have to write the article."

"Technically, no, you don't. But how would that look to your fellow journalists, Susan?"

"As if I were selling out, as guilty as those who took bribes to look the other way."

"Possibly. Not to mention the fact I have no one working for me who can currently write with big-city-paper skill. This issue is going to take careful handling, Susan. And you did get your start here at the *Bugle*, working for my dad and me summers, while you were in college."

Susan grinned, amused by the remark despite the gravity of the situation. "I knew you were going to bring that up."

"Dad always taught me to use every advantage I had when it came to the running of this paper." Patsy leaned back in her chair, surveying Susan thoughtfully. Her expression sobering, she tapped a blue-tipped pencil on the edge of her desk. "You're still worried about how this is going to affect Steve's chances for reelection, aren't you?" She shook her head in wonderment. She looked at Susan as if she were a stranger rather than an old friend.

"Can you blame me? You know how much he wants to be reelected." Susan bit hesitantly into her lower lip. The truth was, she was as inwardly surprised as Patsy. She hadn't expected to ever consider even briefly passing up a plum assignment. Yet the fact remained that if she hadn't owed Patsy in a personal way or felt so strongly about protecting the public in general, she would have simply walked away from the opportunity.

"Look, even if you tried to cover up your part in this, to stay out of the limelight, it wouldn't work. Everyone will know you're responsible."

"How do you figure that? Aren't I guaranteed anonymity for turning them in?"

"Yes, technically, you are. But if the Bruckers were able to get around the inspectors at the health department initially, they may be able to get around this. Obviously they have friends there who are willing to bend the rules slightly, or they never would have been licensed to open and operate the plant. At least not the way it's currently being done."

"So you're saying someone's actually been paid off?" Susan asked. That innocent lives could be at risk so that someone could make a tidier profit margin, infuriated her. She thought of the lavish party the Bruckers had given. How much better it would have been had they channeled some of that money spent back into their food factory, into efforts toward making conditions better for their workers.

"Someone must be taking money on the sly! The only question is who."

Susan shook her head in vexation, counseling, "This isn't Watergate, Patsy. Chances are, no matter what I do or how many people I talk to, I won't be able to find out who actually took the money." Despite Susan's reserved tone, adrenaline was pumping through her veins, making her heart race. She hadn't been this keyed up since she'd left the television station in Lansing.

"No, but you can certainly spur the proper authorities into investigating the matter thoroughly. You're still regarded as a media star here, Susan. And with someone of your television and newspaper experience as a consumer advocate asking that the matter be investigated—"

"They won't dare refuse."

"Exactly. In addition to which, there's a very good chance any article you do write for the *Bugle* may go wire service. Having an article syndicated would help put you back in the limelight," Patsy persuaded. Her eyes narrowed contemplatively. "When you worked at the paper in Cincinnati, you would have given a year's salary for an opportunity like this."

Susan smiled wanly. "Maybe my priorities have changed." Lord, what a mess! She'd started out trying to do a favor for Steve and ended up uncovering a scandal that would undoubtedly rock the town, and maybe the state, before all was said and done.

"So, you'll do it?" Patsy said finally.

"It doesn't seem I have a choice."

Patsy evidently knew enough to quit while she was ahead. "When can I expect the article?" Patsy asked, all business.

With a heartfelt sigh, Susan promised, "I'll start organizing my thoughts tonight. And I'll call you and let you know what happens tomorrow."

AFTER SOME INITIAL BUREAUCRATIC DELAYS, the health officials toured the plant early Wednesday morning. By noon, a closing order had been issued. Patsy's husband, Frank, had the dubious honor of organizing the shutdown. On Thursday, a special issue of the *Taylor County Bugle* was printed. It featured interviews with the enraged plant owners as well as workers. Everyone involved in the Lean Delight manufacturing firm, with the exception of the Bruckers, agreed there were countless problems with the factory setup. But no one was happy about losing a job.

"Well, you should certainly be proud of yourself and all that you've accomplished this week," Patsy told Susan at a press party in her office late Friday afternoon. Members of both wire services plus reporters from several other East Coast papers were in attendance. A television news crew stood by, ready to interview Susan live on the evening news. "Your article was picked up by the wire service. Portions of it are being circulated all over the country. And to top it all off, this recap with the KVUE Action News team may help you get another television job."

As always, directly before airtime, Susan concentrated on keeping her emotions low-key. She was more concerned about her relationship with Steve than resuming her television career. He hadn't been ecstatic to learn they were closing the plant in his absence. "Ready, Ms Trent?" The reporter from the station appeared in the doorway. "We've got the office all set up."

"I'll be right with you." With a smile of anticipation, Susan donned her suit coat and fluffed her hair one last time. It felt good to be working again. She looked forward to her time before the camera. She turned to Patsy. "Wish me luck?"

Patsy grinned and gave her the thumbs-up sign. "Break a leg."

THEY WERE ALREADY COUNTING DOWN to the filming of the spot for the five o'clock news when Steve quietly entered the *Bugle* building via the side entrance. The reception area of the newspaper had been turned into a makeshift studio. Susan, looking polished and professional, was seated in a black vinyl chair against a backdrop of teal-blue broadcloth. She faced an equally sophisticated KVUE reporter. Cameramen and sound technicians had set up near the front door. Because he was in full sheriff uniform, no one thought to question Steve's presence. He stood against the back wall, watching.

The thirty-second cue sounded. Then fifteen. He used the time to observe the woman he had missed all week. Susan was dressed in a black wool pin-striped suit, white silk shirt and red silk tie. She looked very much in her element as the interviewer began after a brief introduction. "With us today is the consumer advocate responsible for breaking the Lean Delight food scandal. Ms Trent, when you toured the factory, did you have any idea Lean Delight frozen dinners were going to be recalled nationwide?''

"No." Briefly, Susan explained how she had come to tour the factory. "It was only after I arrived that I noticed several irregularities." Susan glanced up, past the camera to see Steve. She paused for only a fraction of a second before going on smoothly. "I reported my findings to the health department. They made a surprise inspection. It was at that point they discovered there was an electrical deficiency in one of the heating ovens. Officials knew immediately there was a possibility of salmonella poisoning. Hence, the dinners were recalled." Her heart was pounding. What was he doing there she wondered, and why did he look so displeased? As if by talking on television she had betrayed him personally? He'd been both cordial and accepting on the phone when he'd learned of her involvement. Indeed, he'd encouraged her not only to act but to do so as promptly as possible.

"Do you agree that the plant should be shut down?"

Susan forced her thoughts back to the interview at hand. "Until repairs can be made." Susan's throat was strained, but her voice sounded smooth and well modulated.

"The Bruckers say they have been harassed because they were outsiders here. Do you feel that is true?"

Steve was still watching her steadily. She couldn't see him. She didn't dare look. "In my estimation, the people of Grafton have gone out of their way to welcome the Bruckers," Susan said calmly, refusing to be baited into appearing anything but cool and collected.

"Still, it seems they will leave," the reporter continued. "They've stated that the plant will be closed permanently. How do you feel about that?"

Susan's hands were folded in her lap. Her legs were crossed discreetly at the ankle. "I'm sorry to see the industry go, of course."

"Do you feel any regrets, under the circumstances?"

"I did what any concerned citizen would have done under the circumstances," Susan continued.

The reporter glanced down at the clipboard on her lap and consulted her notes. "In a KVUE interview earlier this morning, the Bruckers hinted Sheriff Steve Markham was behind the plot to have them ousted mainly because they were considering backing another candidate for the sheriff's race. Robert Wakefield has publicly confirmed this as one of several possible motivations on Sheriff Markham's part...."

Susan's eyes sparked to life. Her voice was authoritative as she quashed the thought with a style any politician would have envied. "Nonsense. Sheriff Markham is the most honest, forthright man I know." Susan deliberately avoided looking at Steve.

Steve shifted from his place at the back of the room. He wanted to strangle the KVUE reporter for harassing Susan that way.

The reporter smiled. "Let's examine that in-depth knowledge of yours regarding Sheriff Markham. The two of you are exceptionally close, isn't that right?" the television reporter continued.

"We're...friends." Susan smiled blandly. When she had agreed to the interview, she had no idea it would get so sticky.

"More than that," the KVUE person insisted, leaning forward, her hands clasped over her notes. "Isn't it true the two of you were once engaged?"

"Yes, we were." Susan emphasized the past tense of the verb firmly. She fought to keep the angry, embarrassed color from her face.

"Then how do you explain Sheriff Markham's absence now at such a crucial time, when a deadly blow has just been leveled against the area's economy?"

The KVUE reporter couldn't see Steve coming across the studio from where she sat. By the time the camera and soundmen had reacted, it was too late to stop him from languidly storming the scene. "She doesn't," Steve interjected firmly, walking onto the set before anyone could guess what he was doing. Glad to be out of the hot seat, Susan remained where she was and calmly handed over the mike on her lapel. He pinned it to his khaki shirt, just as she had done earlier. The camera zoomed in on his star and badge while the stunned reporter managed an introduction. "We have with us now Sheriff Steve Markham..."

Steve lifted a hand and waved. "Hello, I'm pleased to be here."

The KVUE reporter was not amused. Oblivious to the interviewer's glare, Steve took the chair a stunned crewman hastily offered. Turning the chair backward, he swung a leg over the seat and sat, his arms folded over the back of the chair. His posture was deliberate, all lazy West Virginia good old boy. The reporter was furious but silent. Steve took advantage of her momentary silence to continue affably, "Just for the record, I've been in Charleston for the state sheriff's conference. The state legislature requires all sheriffs to be present one week every year so that a thorough accounting of crime and our efforts to stop it can be made."

The KVUE reporter queried disbelievingly, "Couldn't you have sent a deputy in to represent the county?"

"Believe me, ma'am, once I found out what was going on here, I tried. But there are no exceptions made unless a county sheriff is desperately ill. And you can see, I'm in perfect health."

The producer signaled thirty seconds to finish. The KVUE reporter regained her equanimity. "That issue aside, you have no qualms about how the Lean Delight scandal was handled?"

"None. Ms Trent's interest in how the factory was run saved unsuspecting consumers from a potential outbreak of food poisoning."

Several more questions were asked and answered. Steve held his own admirably against the aggressive interviewer until time ran out.

The producer made a slashing gesture across his throat. "That's a wrap, folks." Everyone relaxed. Looking as relieved as Susan felt, Steve stood, removed his microphone and handed it to a sound man.

The KVUE reporter protested, "Sheriff, walking on stage, unannounced and uninvited, was clearly—"

"Unprofessional and inconsiderate," Steve broke in. "Sorry if I threw you by appearing so abruptly, but I felt those questions were best answered by me personally. Susan has no more knowledge of my work than I have of hers. Had I known beforehand you were going to film the interview here, I would have requested the chance to be on the show with Susan so the sheriff's department might be better represented.''

''You didn't throw me,'' the disgruntled reporter protested.

''Good.'' Steve flashed a devastating smile. His hand shot out to capture Susan's wrist. He pulled her to her feet. ''I'd like to talk to you. Alone,'' he said quietly. Several reporters, both from television and other newspapers, turned to question Steve. Knowing he was about to receive yet another round of questions, Steve gave them an easy wave. ''I'll answer whatever you need to know later.''

In silence, he and Susan walked outside to his patrol car. He opened the passenger door, waiting until she got in before he circled around the front. Susan smiled. Her heart was racing. She was glad to see him. ''This isn't exactly discreet,'' she teasingly pointed out as he slid behind the weel. Anyone could see them.

For once he didn't tease back. ''You looked very professional just now. I was proud of you,'' he said quietly.

''Thanks.'' His praise made her feel good.

''I understand now why you were so upset at losing the job in Lansing. You were good. Damn good. You belong on television.'' He reached over to hold her hand.

''You mean that?''

''Yes, I do.'' For a moment he was all take-charge sheriff again. ''But that's not why I asked you out here.'' He paused. ''Harvey Brucker came to see me in Charleston this morning. He was furious about what you've done. As the 'man' in your life, he blames me for not having been able to control your actions. When I told him I not only knew about what you planned to do beforehand but supported you completely, he was furious. He's threatened to ruin me.''

Oh, God. She swallowed hard, wetting her lips. ''From the very first I was afraid something like this would happen. I never meant for you to be hurt.''

''I know you didn't. But that won't change what's happened. The Bruckers are claiming my being out of town during the ruckus was no accident, Susan. They're saying to anyone who will listen, including KVUE, I suspect, that I sidestepped the issue to avoid looking bad locally and losing the election. According to them, I'm a coward. At last report, Robert Wakefield and his crew are spreading just the opposite story. They're saying I was paid off *not* to report the health code violations. That if I'd have been here, the plant never would have been either investigated or closed. According to Wakefield, I'm a crook.''

She met his glance compassionately. ''Anyone who knows you realizes neither story is true, especially if they see you on the KVUE evening report.'' Conviction rang true in her voice.

Steve removed his hand from hers and stared out the window at the city street. For several moments he made no effort to share his thoughts with her.

''You're worried you're going to lose now, aren't you?'' Susan said.

''It does seem possible.''

Regret washed over Susan. All at once she felt responsible for all that had happened. Her hand closed over the door handle. "Maybe for your sake it would be best if we didn't see one another until after the election."

He caught her forearm before she could emerge from the car. "You don't mean that."

Susan shrugged. "You heard the KVUE person just now. The local reporters have already made too much of us. I won't be responsible for you losing." Tears of regret sparkled in her eyes. She'd hurt him before inadvertently; she was hurting him again.

"Is that the only reason?"

Susan shrugged. "I want to protect you and give the gossip a chance to die down before people actually go to the polls. It's only two more weeks." She swallowed hard, denying her own desire to spend endless time with him again. "You need to spend the time campaigning without me at your side, damaging your chances by association." Sensing he needed further convincing, she said swiftly, "Look, it's—it's not only that. I've got to work on my book. I've gotten behind on my manuscript since I've been involved in this scandal."

His hand dropped in response to the impersonal tone. His eyes scanned hers a moment longer. "If you change your mind—" he said softly.

Susan nodded her understanding. "Maybe in a few days, after the heat from the investigation cools down...after the Bruckers leave town...when I'm not so busy."

His face took on the rigidness of granite. "I'll wait to hear from you." His tone was curt.

"Steve—"

"I've got to get over to the office, Susan. I need to make a few calls."

"The reporters— You promised—"

"I'll talk to them later." He spoke as if his business were urgent, but he didn't explain. She waited. Still nothing. "Can I give you a lift home?" His tone changed, but was no less distant.

Susan hid her hurt. "No, I've got my car. And I've got some things inside to clear up, too, before I go home." She opened her door.

"I'll see you around, then."

She hastily emerged from the car and walked back into the building. She was left with the definite impression he would not spend much time, if any, waiting for her call.

Susan fumed as she thought about all that had happened. Damn. She couldn't win for losing.

Chapter Ten

No sooner had Susan gotten through the front door of her apartment than a car pulled up in front of the building, followed by roughly a dozen others. She glanced out her window to see Gena Borden marching up her front walk. Fearing the worst, Susan walked out to greet them. "Gena." She nodded stiffly in acknowledgment.

"Hello, Susan."

The group of women looked like a lynch mob. Susan swallowed. Unless she was mistaken, nearly everyone there had been employed at the Lean Delight factory. "Look, I'm sorry about your jobs," Susan began. "I never meant to get anyone laid off."

"But you did close down the plant just the same," Gena countered coolly. She gave Susan a menacing look that took them back to their high-school days. "Susan, we needed those jobs. The pay was better than anything we could have gotten around here. But before you hightail it back into the house, we're not here to talk about something that can't be changed. We're here to ask you to represent us at the mines. They're hiring again at the Taylor County Coal Mine.

Word is they'll be posting names tonight. We want to get there before they make up their lists and remind them that some of us women have been on that waiting list years longer than some of the men.''

Susan forgot her fear and walked on down the steps. "You're saying their hiring practices are unfair?" She was still dressed in the black-and-white ensemble she'd worn for the KVUE interview.

Gena grimaced and lit up a cigarette. "Let's put it this way." She took several puffs and blew out the smoke. "They haven't hired more than two women in the past ten years, and neither of them stayed, they were harassed so much by the men. We aim to change those numbers to a more equitable arrangement. But to do that we have to put pressure on the mine owners. We need media attention, Susan. Public scrutiny of their records and hiring practices. Having you as our spokesperson is the best way to get it."

Back to her celebrity status. Susan sighed. "You owe it to us," Gena Borden calmly pointed out when she saw Susan was wavering.

"I guess I do at that," Susan said. "Just let me go in and change." Jeans and a sweater would be more comfortable.

"No time for that," Gena said, linking arms with her former schoolmate. "We gotta go now, before they realize we're coming."

SUSAN RODE WITH GENA in a beat-up red Dodge Dart. Storm clouds hovered on the darkening horizon. It would be just her luck to have it start to rain, Susan thought. Not that anything like inclement weather would force Gena and the others indoors. "I saw you on television the other night, after they closed down the factory," Gena commented with grudging admiration. She drove, one hand circling the wheel. "You were great with those reporters from the network."

Susan stared out the window at the rough mountainous terrain. She found she could talk to Gena. "I didn't want to go on television." Not initially. Once she'd been back before the camera, though, it had been a different story. It had felt good, almost like going home again. Did Steve realize that, she wondered. Had he seen it, even in the local interview she just did?

Gena shrugged and stepped on the gas pedal harder. "Someone had to go against what the Bruckers were saying, that they were being unfairly harassed." The Dart zoomed around the curve.

"The plant deserved to be closed down, Gena." Glad for her seat belt, Susan's fingers felt for the armrest on the door.

"I know that. Hell, we all did." Gena stamped out her cigarette in the ashtray, then snapped it shut with a bang. "But we've got to make a living. And not all of us want to do it by rolling paper through a typewriter or teaching school." She slanted Susan a commiserating glance. Her tone lowered compellingly. "We've got rights, too, Susan. We just want to see they're protected."

Susan nodded affirmatively in agreement. "I'll do what I can," she promised. Maybe Patsy would run an article in the *Bugle*.

"We're counting on you," Gena said firmly. She slowed her Dodge and guided it past the entrance.

The parking lot was jammed with cars and pick-ups. Already present were several local news crews, both Patsy and her husband, Deputy Frank Winter, and to Susan's dismay, the sheriff's patrol car.

Seeing a grim-faced Steve already talking to several members of Gena's group, Susan swore and fought the urge to slide down in her seat.

"Looks like they're expecting us," Gena reported. "I knew those men would be getting ready to do battle once they realized we were getting organized, too."

Steve turned. He frowned deeply, recognizing Susan, then turned away without a wave or nod of acknowledgment. Susan's heart seemed to stop.

"Sure you're going to be up to this?" Gena asked. She paused, her hand on the door handle.

Susan fought her feelings of anxiety. She supposed that as the head of county law enforcement, Steve could hardly be expected to welcome any journalists to a troubled scene. Still, his unhappy reaction to her stung. She didn't want to do battle with Steve here.

Steve turned toward her again, and she recognized the look of resentment on his face. She grabbed her handbag, rummaged through it swiftly and pulled out a notepad and pen. "I've never let my personal feelings dictate what I write. I'm not about to start now."

Respect was evident in Gena's smile. "Way to go, Susan," she said, giving the thumbs-up sign. "I knew I could count on you." The two women got out of the banged-up car. As soon as Susan locked and slammed the car door, Steve appeared behind her. Before she could turn to face him, his hand shot out to grab her elbow in a viselike grip.

"Excuse us," he said curtly to Gena. "Susan and I have to talk." Susan dug in her heels. He ignored her resistance.

Gena stepped closer and met Steve's glance. Neither won the staring match. Finally, she turned her attention back to Susan and said, "Remember what I said, Susan. You owe this to us."

Susan nodded. She'd been all too willing to help the women before. Steve's possessive attitude only added fuel to her fire. Gena sauntered off.

"We'll talk inside," Steve said stiffly.

"Why not here?" Susan jerked her elbow free of his hold.

"Because what I have to say to you needs to be said in private." He propelled her forcibly up the steps into the rectangular one-story building. Only because she was curious about what was happening inside did Susan offer no resistance to Steve's tactics.

Inside the mining office, a negotiation was going on among men Susan vaguely recognized as mine officials. All conversation stopped as Susan entered the room. After a quick look at Steve, the five men in shirts and ties retreated into another office. Steve ushered her into a small conference room to the left. He shut the door behind them and sat on the edge of the personnel counselor's desk. Susan glanced around, surprised to see the desk conspicuously absent of all paperwork or signs of life. Everything in there had been locked up as tight as a drum, including, she presumed, the large metal file cabinets.

Susan turned back to him at last. She saw the irritation in the set of his mouth. After the way he had manhandled her, she couldn't have cared less. "What the hell are you doing here?'' he demanded through gritted teeth.

Susan folded her arms stiffly across her chest. Her eyes were level with his, as unswerving as her voice. ''The women asked me to help see they get a fair shot at working in the mines. I agreed to do that.''

''Fine.'' He stood, as if the discussion were already finished. ''But do it from behind a typewriter.'' He made as if to show her out.

She was not amenable to being escorted out of the thick of the action. She favored him with an icy smile. ''By then it'll be too late.'' She leaned against the door, blocking his exit.

Hands on her shoulders, he moved her aside. ''At least you'll be safe.'' Again, she barred his way. He swore and shook his head in disgust. His hands reached for her shoulders again and this time didn't let up when she tried to pull away from the restraining action. ''Susan, these men are gearing up for violence.''

''The managers, you mean?'' Susan asked.

His hands dropped. Neither of them moved.

Finally, Steve replied, ''Off the record, yes. They're conferring on just how much action to take. I've advised them to prosecute to the limit anyone arrested for violence.'' His gravelly voice carried a warning.

Susan's excitement rose. It looked as if she had lucked into one hell of a story! ''You think there will be a brawl?''

Steve's mouth thinned derisively. He glanced at his watch. ''First shift will be coming up in roughly another half an hour. Second shift has already been canceled, but the execs expect many of the workers to show up, anyway. When those men find out why the women are here—Susan you know how those men feel about women taking over their jobs in the mine. Currently, in Taylor County, there are three manual laborers for every one position to be filled. An increasing number of women have gone after high-paying jobs. It's a phenomenon many local men resent.''

''Well, that's their problem. Maybe it's time they had their consciousness raised. I'm sorry, Steve. But I can't back down on this simply because a lot of men will have their feelings hurt if a woman beats them out for a position here. Those are the breaks.''

''It's more serious than you realize, Susan. Think about it for a minute. What before would have been only a struggle of an overabundance of workers vying for a small number of jobs now becomes a battle of the sexes, as well. That's a dimension of conflict Taylor County doesn't need.''

''I didn't create the chauvinistic anarchy that fostered the injustice!'' Susan exclaimed.

''No, you didn't. But you're not above turning the turmoil to your own advantage.''

''That's untrue, and you know it,'' Susan shot back. ''I've bent over backward to try to keep my name out of anything controversial going on in this town while your campaign is going on. Why, if I'd wanted to, I could have—''

''What?'' he interrupted furiously when she clamped her mouth shut.

''I could have been a lot more visible than I was,'' she said finally, wishing she'd had the foresight simply to keep her mouth shut and not get dragged into this debate.

"With the media, you mean?"

"Yes," Susan said finally.

He waited a minute, as if mulling over the validity of what she had just said. "What are you doing now? Making up for lost time?"

"You—" She stopped just short of name-calling. It was taking every bit of her self-control not to lash out at him physically.

Steve stepped closer. The essence of might was stamped on him in the authoritative set of his shoulders and the unyielding jaw. "Listen to me, Susan. Go home. Nothing will be solved tonight. You won't miss anything by not being here. I promise you that."

Like hell nothing was going to happen, Susan thought. She could sense the turmoil. It was in the face of everyone present. Coolly, she pointed out, "Victory for the women could be initiated. If so, I feel I ought to be here to record the event properly. There's nothing worse than trying to write an article after the fact, when the only information you have is based on hearsay or personal opinions."

Ten seconds passed. Steve's jaw was rigid. "The only thing that will come of tonight is more violence. No one here needs that. Least of all you, Gena Borden or her friends."

"Why don't you let me be the judge of what I need?" she said directly. Susan wasn't about to be railroaded. Steve sighed deeply, as if exhausted, and tried to assess the situation more clearly.

Comprehension dawned slowly. "Is this where you were headed when you left the paper this afternoon?'' He knew, she thought, with renewed annoyance. All along he knew this was going to happen, and he didn't tell her. He was deliberately keeping information from her that he knew she'd be interested in both professionally and personally.

"I got word earlier, before I left Charleston, they were expecting a near-riot.''

"I see." Her deep sense of betrayal was evident in her tone. She shrank back against the door, then turned to go.

"No, you don't." His low voice whispered across her neck. Unbidden, she turned partway toward him. From the outer office came a new rumble of voices, both men's and women's. She ignored them, as did he, momentarily concentrating on what he had to say. "This encounter could turn out to be very dangerous. We've alerted other area law-enforcement agencies. They're standing by now, ready to come if we need them. Damn it, Susan," he whispered very low, "I don't want to see you get hurt.''

The raw emotion in his voice affected her like no angry words ever could have. "I'll stay well out of the way of any violence," she promised. "All I want to do is watch and record what's happening so I can do it again later for the paper.''

He shook his head negatively. His lips were compressed tightly. He took her by the shoulders, but this time his grasp was gentle, compelling. "You won't be able to avoid the brawling. No one here will, once it gets started.''

His position was beginning to make sense. "I've got an obligation to stay and see this through, Steve. I owe those women after what happened." She expected him to understand.

"Your only obligation is to yourself," he countered. "And maybe to me. For once, Susan, think of what I need from you."

"I am thinking of you," she protested. "But I also know firsthand what it feels like to be unemployed, with little prospect of gaining employment in your chosen field. Those women are being unfairly treated. You know it, and I know it."

He said nothing. "Tonight won't solve anything."

"Maybe, maybe not. But those women don't stand a chance to get hired unless they do stand up for themselves. Do you realize what you're doing by asking me to go home? You're asking me to sacrifice my principles." She made no effort to mask her outrage.

"I'm asking you to consider my feelings!"

"Damn it, I have considered your feelings." They were on the verge of shouting at one another. How would that look? Her voice lowered. She swallowed with difficulty, then tried one last time to reason with him. "Steve, please. I can't change my mind. Don't push this."

He was tempted to shake her. His hands raised, then dropped in a gesture of frustration. "Susan, we're doing our best to control this situation, but there are never any guarantees." He enunciated the words carefully. The week away from her had been stressful, the television interview not exactly a piece of cake. He hadn't wanted to deal with this, too. "I want you to go home."

She exhaled exasperatedly. "I can't do that." She pleaded. "Why won't you understand?"

He didn't move; abruptly, he seemed a thousand miles away emotionally. "I won't be responsible for what happens if you stay."

"Meaning what?" Her hand searched for the doorknob. Her shoulder wedged against the door.

"Meaning just that."

She yanked open the door, ignoring the obvious stares of several television cameramen and the same KVUE reporter who had interviewed Susan at five o'clock. She turned back to Steve, hissing in a barely audible whisper, "You've said what you had to say. I've listened."

He chortled quietly. "Did you?" His brows raised mockingly.

She ignored his last remark, continuing as if he hadn't spoken at all. "Now, I want you to leave me alone."

She strode defiantly toward the building exit. The KVUE reporter followed, a microphone clutched in her hand. Susan, aware of Steve's disapproving gaze upon her, not only consented to an interview; she personally led the KVUE crew out to talk to Gena and others who'd been fired from Lean Delight.

During the next half hour several more news crews arrived. The first shift of the mine let out. Learning why the women were there, the men became openly challenging and abusive, verbally threatening the women with violence if they so much as tried to step foot in the mines. Gena stated her complaint before the cameras. Susan, acting as spokesperson for the group, elaborated on her remarks, offering general information about Grafton, the women there, the lack of both job opportunities for women and high-paying jobs. The men countered with their view that no woman was physically capable of the work. To the laughter of the network personnel, Gena stepped in front of the cameras and offered to arm wrestle anyone there. Only Frank Winter's intervention prevented a conflict.

Steve stood off to the side, watching carefully. So far no arrests had been made, because the mine owners didn't want trouble. But their hopes that the excitement would die down and everyone would leave once the people realized jobs weren't going to be posted were not materializing. From a distance, Susan looked unaffected by the tension lacing the crowd. When she wasn't talking to a newsperson, she was scribbling notes hastily on the pad of paper in her hand. Steve had the same recurring thought: he wished she would go home. He decided abruptly to give it one last try.

Handing the bullhorn over to Frank, he threaded his way through the crowd. He found Susan talking to Gena. He drew her over to the side. "Had enough?" His voice was angry. "Or haven't you been on television enough for one day?" That she looked undeniably lovely and poised only added to his smoldering fury.

She flashed him a confident smile and tossed her head. The rumble like atmosphere evidently excited her. "I'll leave when it's over."

She didn't seem to want his opinion. He wondered how fast she would remain brave if the confrontation did get violent. "If you do, it'll be in the back of a paddy wagon," he threatened. She smiled again and started to walk away. He grabbed her arm, wishing even as he acted that he hadn't given in to the involuntary action.

"You don't have any say in this," she said.

How well he knew that. "Don't expect any favors from me later," he warned. He hated feeling powerless. To be made to look like a fool in front of the whole community was worse. He was the sheriff. He ought to be able to handle one woman. He ought to be able to handle Susan. But he never had been able to dissuade her when she was working.

Susan regarded Steve stonily. He looked impossibly handsome in the starched uniform, his hair windtossed, cheeks ruddy from the wind. More than his strength, she needed his ability to compromise and make everyone look like a winner. But his ability to mediate had been lost. He wanted an end to the confrontation. Nothing less than immediate compliance would satisfy him, and that she couldn't give. Susan turned away.

Then he gave up. "Have it your own way." He strode back toward the mine management.

Susan was left, aching with hurt, wishing for the simple love they had shared before he'd left for Charleston nearly a week before. Was that all they would ever have, she wondered.

By dark the situation had worsened. Gena was squaring off against the owner of the mine. Namecalling was the least of it; any second Susan expected to see fists fly. And that's when Steve stepped in, bullhorn in hand. Calmly, he advised everyone to go home. No one moved. The women linked hands, unexpectedly including Susan in the middle of the line next to Gena, encouraging her to stay when she balked. The men lined up opposite them as cameras from network and cable companies filmed busily. The building quartering the mine executives had been thoroughly roped off; it was guarded by both Grafton police and the Taylor Mine's security men. Glancing back at the men opposite the women, Susan was filled with the hysterical desire to laugh. The squaring off reminded her of a childhood game, "Red Rover." But the stakes here were much higher. Crossing the line of men blocking the entrance to the mine office could be dangerous. Her anxiety increased as she saw several men remove flasks from their pockets and drink from the small containers.

Her hands trembled. She held tight to Gena. "Look, Susan, if you want to go home now, we'll all understand," Gena whispered. Nearby, rival news crews were filming steadily, each one wanting to capture the first moment of violence.

Gena's pity for Susan's fear was evident.

Susan pulled herself together and shook her head vigorously. "No. I've seen it through this far. I'm staying until the end, Gena." She would write an article for Patsy. She would write several, hopefully for eventual publication all around the United States.

Paddy wagons rolled through the front gates of the mine. Men in police uniform got out. Gena swore beneath her breath. Steve picked up his bullhorn one last time. He repeated his order that they disperse at once. The police officers moved between the lines of men and women. When no one moved, the arrests started. First to be taken away were the men who'd been drinking. Gena and Susan were next.

From the way Steve had been glaring at her during the showdown, Susan had half expected Steve to rescue her personally, to take her to jail in his patrol car. She got half her wish. Cameras clicking, television cameras whirring, he strode forward to read her her rights.

Susan took a deep breath, trying to contain her anger at having been arrested for such a ridiculous reason. Some of the women and men verbally urged her to resist.

Moments later, Robert Wakefield moved through the crowd. "What? No special treatment for your woman, sheriff? You disappoint me!" His tone was condescending. He made it look as if Steve were secretly giving Susan an out, instead of arresting her, when they all knew he would never do anything of the kind.

"Steve doesn't make exceptions," Susan shot back, unable to help herself. Damn it, she had to come to his defense. She couldn't stop her involuntarily protective reaction. She wouldn't let Robert twist her involvement in the mine company trouble to his own advantage. "Everyone here knows that."

"Everyone here is waiting to see," Robert corrected.

Steve clamped a hand over Susan's elbow. He shot Robert a mild look. "Get out of here, Wakefield, and do it now or you'll be arrested along with the rest." Steve's countenance was unwaveringly grim.

"I'm going." Robert held both hands up in a surrendering gesture. There was a ripple of questions from reporters. Robert backed off, only too glad to answer their questions, while at the same time handing out campaign brochures and announcing to one and all how if he had been sheriff the whole confrontation would never have occurred. Susan was willing to bet that as self-serving as Robert seemed, if he'd been sheriff, the disagreement would have resulted in chaos unlike anything Taylor County had ever seen.

Aware of the cameras clicking all around, Steve took her arm and steered her toward the waiting paddy wagon. Susan dragged her heels. His grip on her arm increased. There was no change in his expression. Chaos was all around them as others were being similarly arrested. "You're hurting me," she complained, still struggling mildly.

"Not half as much as I'd like to," he retorted.

"If you want a scene—"

He stopped so fast she stumbled into his chest. "Yes?" His brows raised mockingly.

"You'll get it." She pressed her fists against his chest, wedging distance between them. She could feel his heart pounding just as quickly as her own. Only with great restraint was she able to keep herself from childishly stomping on his toes.

"Here? How public! How stupid!" He removed her hands from his chest as he would have swatted away a pesky fly. Maintaining a firm hold on her arm, he growled, "If you don't care about me, think about your folks and what a resisting-arrest charge will do to them."

It was not the threat of her parents' wounded feelings but the words "if you don't care about me" that made her go numb. She was silent, almost acquiescent as he backed her up against the paddy wagon.

He was too close to her. The fiery heat of his body penetrated her chilled bones. A tremor of exhaustion added to her chill.

"When this is all over, we're going to talk," he warned gruffly.

"About what?" she snapped back. Her heart was still pounding. She was furious with him but glad he'd been the one to initiate her arrest. The truth of the matter was, during the demonstration she'd been frightened for both Steve and herself. Now she wanted the whole fiasco over as quickly as possible.

"About us," he delineated fiercely. Without another word, he strode back toward the crowd and his obligations.

Deputy Frank Winter herded Susan into the back of the paddy wagon. "You know you're going to have a criminal record now, don't you?" Frank said with a sigh as she sat down gingerly on the narrow seat.

With Steve out of the immediate area, Susan began to relax. She was annoyed, as much at her own short-sightedness as at the prospect of having her fingerprints registered with the FBI. "That ought to look great on my job applications. Any chance the mining company will drop the charges?" she asked hopefully.

Frank Winter replied, "Not a one. If they did let even one person go without official and permanent reprimand, it would encourage this sort of thing to happen again. No, you can bet there'll be stiff fines and penalties for everyone arrested tonight. That's why I made Patsy go home when you were in the mine office with Steve. If you had been smart, you would've listened to him then."

"Patsy wanted to stay?" Susan had wondered where she had run off to.

"You bet. But I wouldn't let her," Frank stated.

"Wouldn't?" Susan bristled at his tone, watching as Frank seated another woman across from her.

"That's right, wouldn't," Frank retorted contentiously. "In this she obeys me or else." His tone softened. "I told her to think of the kids."

"And that did it?"

"Yes."

Susan watched him retreat, mystified. Was that what Steve had expected of her, too? Blind obedience?

Gena, not about to be reasonable, struggled and resisted arrest. It took three men to lift her into the wagon. By the time they finished, her hair was tangled, her face dirty and bruised. Never had Susan seen her look happier. "Some protest, huh, Susan?" Gena said. Susan felt it was only the beginning.

The ride to jail was the longest journey Susan had ever taken in her life. Packed into the back of the police wagon like sardines, they were confined and uncomfortable. The mood of the women, however, was victorious. "Did you see those news cameras?" Gena exhorted. "There's no way they can ignore us now."

Susan agreed. "We'll follow up the protest with letters to the appropriate government agencies, send telegrams to congressmen, notify the American Civil Liberties Union." Which was, she thought ruefully, probably what they should have done in the first place. What if Steve hadn't been on top of the situation as he had—going in early, having the foresight to notify other law-enforcement agencies in the area? What if the situation had gotten truly out of hand? With the men drinking, the confrontation could have been much more serious.

She thought of Steve's anger, the way he had looked at her in contempt. Misery engulfed her.

"Ever been to jail?" Gena asked.

Susan shook her head.

Gena sighed and rubbed at her bruised jaw with the edge of one handcuffed hand. "Well, you're in for a real treat."

Chapter Eleven

"Cheer up," Gena Borden advised. "It could be worse." Thirty women had been crowded into a twelve-by-sixteen cell meant for eight. They'd been in the lockup for five hours. To Susan, it felt like five years.

"I don't see how it could be worse," Susan grumbled. She rested her face against the bars, wishing for fresh air, a bath and a decent meal, all of which she'd gone far too long without.

Gena shrugged and laughed. "You could have a resisting-arrest charge after your name, too."

Susan straightened and leaned against the bars. Never one for getting much exercise, she found herself wanting to run at least ten miles, nonstop. "True. I did go along quite nicely, didn't I?"

Gena nodded agreeably. "Too nicely for my taste. But what the hell, anyone could see you were scared."

"I was not! Well, maybe a little. At first." She grinned, confessing in rueful tones, "When it looked as if the Red Rover game was about to turn into Charge!"

"Wouldn't that have been something if they had tried to break through our line," Gena said. Her face was lit with a distracted smile.

Susan shook her head in resignation. Exhausted, many of the others were asleep, curled up wherever they could find the space. Gena seemed to have plenty of energy left. "This really doesn't bother you, does it, Gena? Being cooped up in here like a—a—"

"Prisoner."

"Prisoner." Misery washed over Susan, making her want to retch. At the rear of the cell was a basin and a commode. Located out in the open, neither bathroom fixture afforded one with the least privacy.

Gena paced back and forth. "At least we didn't get searched and sprayed for lice."

Susan shuddered at the thought, asking curiously, "You have?" Susan had learned she could ask Gena anything without fear of offending her. She liked that.

"Sure. I was in the juvenile detention center over in Clarksburg a lot when I was a kid." Gena looked up at the ceiling. Several spiderlike cracks spread through the aging light green paint.

"I remember you missing a lot of school." Susan watched her, fascinated. She sat down next to the bars, drawing her knees up to her chest while still retaining as much modesty as possible by smoothing the skirt up along her thighs.

"That was why. I was always in one scrape after another." Gena held two fingers to her lips; she obviously wanted a cigarette. But smoking was out of the question. "I grew up in a tough neighborhood. My father roughed me up a lot. I was always running away."

Gena asked for no sympathy. Susan didn't burden her with any. "Do you see your folks much now?" If Gena accepted her situation baldly, so could she.

Gena shook her head negatively. "No. My father died a couple years ago in a fight outside a bar." She sighed, looking pensive. "My mother left a long time ago."

"Do you have any brothers and sisters?" Susan took off her shoes and wriggled her toes. Perdition, but her feet ached.

Gena brightened. "Two brothers in the navy. A sister that's married to a man just like my father."

"Why would she do that?" Susan asked. "Marry someone who's liable to abuse her?"

Gena shrugged. She looked at Susan, for the first time with a hint of envy. "'Cause where I come from, some men think it's their right. That's one of the reasons I wanted to work in the mines so bad. To show the male chauvinist pigs women aren't any different. We're sure not weaker." Gena cast a disparaging glance at Susan's lack of muscle. "Most of us, anyway."

Susan grinned. Since no offense was meant, none was taken. "You've never been married or anything?" She rubbed at her arches, massaging away the tension. It was three in the morning, and the jail had grown almost peaceful.

Gena replied. "No. Lived with a man for a while. Decided I wasn't going to clean up after anyone but myself. When he found out maid service didn't come with the place, he took off. I was glad to see him go."

"The confrontation tonight didn't scare you?"

"Sure." Gena stood again, as anxious to be out of there as Susan had been earlier. She stretched languorously before saying, "The prospect of getting beat up scares everyone. But you can't let that stop you from fighting for what you believe in."

Gena was every bit the feminist Susan was, only more militant, Susan realized. She propped her chin on her knees. "Would you mind if I do an article on this—on you specifically—when we get out?"

Gena made no effort to veil her wariness. "Why?"

"Because I think it might help keep public pressure on the mines to hire more women, to make their hiring practices more fair. And because I'd like other women to understand your reasons for being there tonight."

"I wouldn't mind. You know, Susan, you're okay."

"Thanks, Gena." Susan stood, and they shook hands. "You're not half bad yourself."

Susan spent the rest of the night interviewing the other women in the cell. By the time they were hauled into court at ten the next morning, she had quite a collection of information written in the small notepad tucked inside her suit-coat pocket.

Sentencing was swift and uniform for all the men and women involved in the riot. Steve was withdrawn throughout the proceedings. He didn't glance at Susan once. When she was on her way out of the courtroom, however, he caught her arm. "Just a moment," he said very low. "I want to talk to you."

Susan winced. Her every defense snapped to attention. "What about?"

"Upstairs in my office. I'll meet you there in ten minutes." He disappeared to talk to the judge without giving her a chance to comment.

Susan stood there indecisively. She smelled horrible. Her clothes were filthy and stained with dirt and perspiration. She wanted a shower, then a good night's sleep, some clean clothes and something to eat. But before any of that, she wanted to type up the article for the *Bugle*. The article was important, and she wanted people to be able to read it before they forgot about the riot at the mine.

Still, she found herself climbing the stairs to the third floor after receiving her personal belongings from the temporary clerk assigned to the hall adjacent to the Taylor County courtroom. Ducking into the restroom, she washed her face, combed her hair and applied some lipstick. A spray of perfume helped boost her morale.

When she finally walked into Steve's office, he was waiting for her, looking furious. Quietly, she closed the door behind her. "Have a seat."

Normally, Susan would have ignored any instruction given her in such a demanding tone. Deciding she was too tired to tangle with him, she started for the chair in front of his desk.

"Not that one." His icy voice stopped her dead in her tracks.

She pivoted toward him, the pulse hammering in her neck. He continued with a sweeping arm movement that mocked even as it directed. "Take the chair behind the desk. That is where you'd like to be, isn't it, Susan? In a position of power and visibility?"

Her temper was rising. Again, Susan decided to let his remark pass. She shrugged, not about to let him know how much he was getting to her. "Have it your own way." She seated herself behind his desk, crossed her legs, tipped the chair back and folded her hands in her lap. Her chin lifted defiantly. She waited.

He stalked over to the coffee maker, poured her a cup of coffee, stirred in cream and handed it to her with amazing civility. Susan's uneasiness increased. She took it, sipping the strong hot liquid. She shouldn't have come, she realized belatedly. She should have gone home. He paced with deceptive indolence toward the file cabinet in the corner. She felt about as safe as she would if she were locked in a cage with a hungry mountain lion. "Have you read the morning paper?" he asked with grating pleasantness. "Of course not. How could you after having spent the night in jail."

That did it. Susan was up and out of her chair in a second and a half. "I don't have to listen to this."

"Sit down." A muscle worked convulsively in his cheek. "I want you to see these, Susan. Now." His tone indicated he was not to be disobeyed. Telling herself for the moment it was easier to comply than to fight, she sat, but this time on the edge of her chair. Unceremoniously, he tossed her the first paper. The *Charleston Telegram*. A picture of Susan was front and center. In the photo, Steve was dragging Susan away by the arm. Actually, Susan thought, it wasn't a half-bad picture of her, considering. The caption read, "West Virginia Sheriff Arrests Television Reporter."

"Well," she shrugged uncaringly, "it could have been worse."

"Read the article." The words were spit out like shards of glass. Curiously, Susan glanced through the melodramatic prose, cringing several times. "They didn't leave much out, did they? How did they find out we were once engaged, I wonder? Or that we'd been seeing one another again."

"Robert Wakefield, no doubt. Does it matter?" Turning, he lifted down another stack of papers. One by one, they flopped onto the desk. All alluded to the fact that she had recently been employed by WJCG in Lansing, Michigan. "My favorite is the article in the *Cincinnati Enquirer*." Susan laughed, pointing to the quotation: "Consumer Advocate Finds New Battles to Fight, in Life as Well as Love. They probably did that just because I used to work there."

"Your picture and mine are in nearly every paper statewide. I've had calls all morning from other sheriffs I met at the conference last week, telling me about it. Some of them have even read the articles over the phone. Between bursts of laughter, of course."

Susan refused to pacify him. "Of course."

He made no reply, but simply stared at her over the rim of his coffee cup. He was clenching the cup with both hands. His eyes were bloodshot and tired.

Susan tried to think of something positive to say, some good that had come out of the mess the previous evening. Finally, she offered, "At least you're shown enforcing law and order. I'm shown breaking the law." And she was still in the process of searching for a job. Susan groaned audibly, cradling her head in her hands.

"And yet you somehow manage to emerge a heroine. Was that your plan, Susan? To garner a little free publicity for yourself while ruining everything I've worked for here?"

She took another sip of coffee. Okay, he was upset, he was tired, and he was overreacting. After the night they had suffered, he was entitled. As his friend and a woman who loved him, she would hear him out. Calmly, she tried to reason with him. "I don't know what you're talking about."

"Don't you!" He took a step nearer, leaned forward, his hands flat on the desk. Physical restraint vibrated from him, making her shrink back slightly in her chair. "You've made it clear you care for me and want our affair to continue indefinitely. You also plan to leave the city. How convenient if I'm forced out of office at the same time you wrangle yourself a new job somewhere else."

It was an effort to keep her voice calm. Somehow she managed. "I never planned any such thing."

"Maybe not consciously!" he shot back.

"Not at all! Damn it, you know that's not true. I believe in the battle those women are waging!" She almost cited the additional information she'd gained during the lockup, then decided against it. No doubt he'd be furious if he knew she intended to continue her fight, too, by writing a series of in-depth articles.

He moved away from the desk with calculated slowness. "And not once last night did it occur to you that your presence there alone was guaranteed to make me look like a fool!"

"It occurred to me you'd be angry with me." Because she had no defense for his other accusation, she refused to address it.

He jammed his hands in his pockets and leaned back against the wall. There was both an urgency about his anger and a desperation that disturbed her greatly. He was acting as if it were all over between them. Why? Was he that hurt? "How many of the people around here do you think are going to vote for a sheriff who can't even control his own woman?" She uncoiled from the chair and stood, sore from a night spent in cramped quarters. She moved closer, her commitment to him showing in her eyes. He knew she loved him, she thought. She always had and always would.

There was truth to what he was saying, she knew. But it was an antiquated notion that shouldn't be allowed to persist. "Your woman, Steve? I don't belong to anyone."

"Well, you've sure as hell made that perfectly clear, haven't you." He was acting like some macho version of a caveman. Suddenly, she recalled the only other time he had acted as irrationally; it was the day he had broken up with her in Lansing.

She sighed in exasperation, summoning what little patience she had left. "The people know you don't have any control over what I do, say or think." She wouldn't let him leave her again over something that trivial. They would find a way to work it out together.

"Sure, they know it. You just proved it!"

Tears burned inside her. She refused to let them fall. "I'm sorry if you think I've...hurt your chances for being reelected. That was not my intention, believe me." Her voice was as soft and low as she could make it.

With effort, Steve controlled his temper. He shook his head and voiced what had been nagging at him all night. "Susan, you could have been hurt there."

"I wasn't." She closed the distance between them, her face upraised.

Steve studied her silently. Even after the hell she'd been through, she was the loveliest and most earnest woman he had ever known. Almost involuntarily, his hand reached out to curve against her face. Her skin was soft as satin beneath the calloused roughness of his palm. "You could have been hurt," he repeated. His hand dropped to his side. He studied the flag on the opposite wall. "Do you think I could have forgiven myself if you'd gotten hit with a bottle or a rock?"

"I wasn't."

"No, you weren't. You also didn't trust me enough to abide by my assessment of the situation." His anger was genuine, and it wouldn't go away.

She pivoted and walked toward the window. The street below was exceptionally quiet. The news crews and trucks that had flooded the town the day before were long gone, probably onto their next story. "An assessment that proved wrong."

"It's never going to work between us, is it?" The lack of sleep gnawed at him. Much as he wanted to, he couldn't contain his fury or his hurt. "You're always going to be chasing after some damn story."

Hands on her waist, Susan turned to face him. She looked as poised at that moment, as in control, as she ever had on television. He both respected and resented her for it. "Maybe I will be. Just like you're always going to feel a responsibility to uphold and obey the law, no matter what. That doesn't mean that we can't find a way to be together." They faced one another in silence.

His disgruntled mood stayed with him. "Temporarily, maybe." His pronouncement was full of scorn. "Unless I decided to chuck everything and move with you to the next stage of your career. Right?"

Susan didn't want to even think about that. She closed her eyes briefly.

In the sunlight she looked pale and tired. There were faint shadows beneath her eyes that makeup couldn't cover.

"Don't twist things around."

He remembered how much of a stranger she had become when she'd moved to Lansing. Were they headed for the same self-absorption again? If he hadn't been able to handle it before, how would he deal with it now? Why did his wanting her always make him feel like such a bastard? Was that the way it was when a man was in love with a woman or merely a sign he needed to get out of the relationship fast, for her sake as much as his?

Angrily, he continued. "And what should I do? Act like nothing happened last night? Act like I don't know you're using me and this situation here as some sort of stepping-stone to fame?" He knew that was untrue the moment he said it; the hurt look on her face confirmed it. But once the words were out, he wouldn't take them back.

Susan abruptly looked just as glacial. "We made promises to each other we weren't able to keep before, Steve. I don't want to do that again."

"You're right, of course." He had agreed to go slow. A week after making love to her again, he was searching for the happily ever after.

She had the feeling he despised her.

Steve determined to do better at keeping his distance, at least for a while, until he had his own feelings better under control. There was no point in hurting her unnecessarily. He willed himself an emotional anesthetic. "Do you need a ride home?"

"No." She wanted to go across the street and down the block to the *Bugle* first. She wanted to talk to

Patsy, and she didn't want Steve to know about it. She ran a hand through her hair in an agitated gesture. She had never meant to hurt him. He needed to know that. "Look, about your campaign. If you want me to, I'll make some sort of formal statement about our present relationship." It was the only way she knew to help at that point, as the damage had already been done.

"No." His face was closed and unreadable. His hands clenched with the effort not to touch her. "Just...go. I'll see you later."

She didn't want to leave it like this between them, unsettled, with both of them hurting and silent. They had parted like that before, but there seemed to be no way to get through the barriers he'd erected. She smiled weakly, attempting a joke. "You definitely will see me later. After all, I've got a new community-service fine to serve out, as does everyone else arrested last night."

The standard sentence had been fifty hours. Those charged with resisting arrest like Gena had been given another fifty hours, making their total one hundred hours.

"You can take the papers with you."

"No, thanks."

Never had a conversation with a woman been more awkward for him, less satisfactory. He held open his outer office door. "I don't want them." It was ridiculous for him to resent so much her time in the limelight. But he did.

"All right." Unwillingly, she picked up the stack of papers and slid them under her arm. She turned toward him hesitantly. "Steve—"

He wouldn't hear her out. "No more talk, Susan. I haven't got time. If you want to do something constructive, stay away from my campaign headquarters for a few days, at least until the furor dies down.''

She could understand his being upset. She was sorry she'd hurt his chances for reelection. She was even sorrier her picture and his and the titillating story had made the front page of every paper on the East Coast, but she wasn't regretful. ''Can I call you?'' she asked softly.

Steve hesitated. He was making their situation even worse with his sulking. He needed time to get his feelings under control again. ''No. I'll call you.''

The promise sounded like a cliché. She laughed, but tears sparkled in her eyes. ''Right, Steve. You've made your point. I'm no longer welcome in your life.'' She gave him a moment. He didn't contradict her.

She hadn't wanted to renew their love affair, he reminded himself. When she had first returned to Grafton, she had warned him the move was only temporary. If he was hurting now, wanting more than she was prepared to offer him, it was his own fault.

Head held high, she walked past him, out the door. He did nothing to stop her departure. He couldn't. The thought of losing her again hurt too much.

Chapter Twelve

"Didn't I always tell you hard work is rewarded?" Susan's father said several days later. It seemed a lifetime since she had seen or heard from Steve.

Susan sat down on the sofa. She slipped off her coat and gloves. "Yes, Dad, you did. And the job offer from the Minneapolis television station is everything I've been looking for." She'd been so excited when the station manager had called, inviting her up for an interview, she'd hardly been able to contain her exuberance. Her first thoughts had been of Steve. She'd instinctively wanted to share the good news with him. Thinking better of it, she had thrown on her coat and rushed over to her parents' home instead. Cheerily, she continued to fill her parents in on all that had happened. "The hours are good, only five days a week. The salary is excellent. The audience is smaller than the one I had in Lansing, but on the other hand, it is a job, and it's in the field I want to work in." From there, given time and more experience, she could always move up again.

"What does Steve say about the offer?" Emma Trent asked. She looked up from the art project she was organizing for her kindergarten class. Beneath the folding table she had set up, bits of colored construction paper littered the floor.

Susan walked over and absently picked up the colored remnants, tossing them into the wastepaper basket. She dusted off her hands and avoided her mother's scrutiny. "I haven't told him yet."

"Oh?" Emma's eyebrows rose. She exchanged a worried look with Clayton.

Susan bit back a torrent of defensive words, saying only, "I haven't seen him since the day I was arrested. But I'm going to have to." She walked back to the sofa and sat down. She picked up her driving gloves and twisted them in her hands. "The job in Minneapolis is only available if I take it within the next month. I have to give them an answer by November fifteenth, and start work approximately a month after that." One month to decide. The deadline sounded punishing because it meant the end of her time in Grafton, the end of her reprieve from the pressures of work. The end of her time with Steve.

"Why, that wouldn't give you any time at all," Emma sympathized. Finishing up she began collecting similar-sized pieces of brightly colored Thanksgiving turkeys and securing them with rubber bands.

"I know. I'd have to leave before Christmas if I were to take that job." She thought about Christmas without Steve, without her folks. Despair washed over her. Susan put her gloves aside and stared down at the floor, desperate for her parents not to see the tears suddenly burning in her eyes. She hadn't wanted her time in Grafton to end so miserably, with her relationship with Steve in even worse straits than when she had arrived. How had she ever imagined they could be friends again? How had she let them become lovers, only to end it again with razorlike swiftness? As much as she tried to deny or hide it, her heart ached with the loss.

Silence fell in the room.

"Will you be able to fulfill your community-service obligation?" Clayton asked. He put down his evening paper and granted his daughter his full attention.

"Yes, but I'll have to work out a deal that will enable me to complete my commitment sooner than scheduled. As it is now, they've got me working alternate Saturdays, a few hours at a time, for the next six months. Which is another reason I have to see Steve." Susan stood, sliding her hands into the pockets of her skirt. "I'm going to have to get his cooperation to work out my scheduling problems. Hopefully, he'll be cooperative and put in a good word for me with the judge." She was being unreasonably optimistic, she knew. She was also using the scheduling problem as an excuse to see Steve again. She could make an appointment and see the judge alone. She wanted somehow to get talking again, and if pretending to need his help more than she actually did would at least get them on the road to recovery, that would be it.

Clayton grimaced. "I wouldn't count on Steve helping you out in this if I were you."

Susan paced restlessly, turned and took a deep breath. "I know what you mean, Dad. Steve's still fairly irascible with me now. Maybe if you talked to him…" She left the thought hanging in hopes Clayton would pick it up and volunteer to intervene on her behalf. No such luck. Her father was as determined to mind his own business as always and let her fight her own battles.

One look into her mother's face told Susan that she echoed her husband's sentiment. This was one time she didn't want their encouragement toward independence. Before she could speak, Clayton cut her off firmly, saying, "This is between you and Steve. However the two of you work it out, you'll have to do it alone, with no outside interference."

Susan's heart ached as she recalled the detached way he had looked at her that morning when she'd left his office. "But he's not even speaking to me at the moment!" Susan persisted.

"Maybe he just needs to hear you say you're sorry," Emma suggested, barely looking up from the art project she was organizing.

"Me!" Susan nearly shouted. For emphasis, she thumped her chest with her open palm. "He's the one who arrested me! Gave me a criminal record!"

"Only after you broke the law," Clayton pointed out. "Face it, Susan. You made a mistake, a big one, when you went after that story with no restraint. You got what you wanted, a great series of articles, another job in television. But personally, you're going to have to pay for the predicament and heartache you've caused for Steve, and frankly I think it's only fair you suffer a little, too."

"Dad! How can you take that position with your own daughter!"

He waved off her protests. "Very easily. But you're right; I think we have said enough, indeed too much, on this subject." Her father paused, adding more gently, "Go see Steve, Susan. Work it out, or at least try. You owe each other that much."

Susan knew her father was right about seeing Steve. And after worrying nearly all night about how Steve would react both to her uninvited presence and the job offer she had just received, she finally went to see him early the next morning. She caught him in his courthouse office. He was drinking coffee, going over the reports from the previous evening, when she entered his office.

Unable to broach the job offer at first, she began with her desire to speed up the serving of her community-service fine. "I'd like to work off my debt to the community this month."

"Why the rush?"

Susan hedged.

He crossed his arms over his chest. "If you don't level with me and tell me the truth, there's not a chance in this world I'll help you."

Susan swore. Haltingly, she explained the Minneapolis television offer.

"Are you taking the offer?" His tone was clipped.

"I don't know yet."

"What about your book?" Steve asked curtly.

"I'm almost done with the book. I'm typing the final draft now." She let out a wavering breath at his stony expression. "That's another reason I'd like to work off my debt full-time. It will fill up the empty hours."

"You're that close to being finished with your book?" Steve asked.

He had hoped that project would keep her there indefinitely. He should have known Susan would breeze through a project like that in record time after her years as a newspaper and television journalist.

Susan nodded affirmatively. "I'll probably be done today or tomorrow. I'll have revisions to do, of course, once my editor reads the manuscript, but those won't be in for quite a while."

He contemplated her request briefly. He went with his gut reaction. "No way am I helping you arrange your community-service fine so you can take another job out of state."

She hadn't expected him to be ecstatic for her, but she'd hoped he would at least be polite. "I haven't even decided to take the job yet! I just want to get my sentence over sooner."

"Whether you take that particular job or not isn't the issue. I resent your evasiveness, your unwillingness to discuss or confront anything I might be unhappy about. The fact is, you want to leave Grafton. Be honest, Susan. You can't wait to get away from here." He moved away from his desk. His chair made a grating sound on the floor. Hands jammed into his pockets, he stalked to the window. Muted sounds of light traffic could be heard from the street below.

"That's not true." Susan swallowed around the knot in her throat. Her heart was pounding. How could he think her so unfeeling, she wondered, when just the thought of leaving Steve again was tearing her apart? Couldn't he see how torn up she was? Or didn't he want to? Heaven knew, in the whole time she'd been in his office, he seemed not the least bit receptive to anything she had to say.

A fathomless silence descended. With effort, Susan remained seated. She tugged her skirt down over her knees. She had dressed carefully, spending more time than usual on her hair and makeup. She could see the extra effort was having the opposite of the desired effect on Steve. Instead of not being able to take his eyes off her, he seemed hardly able to look at her.

Steve continued to stare into space. At her vaguely hopeful glance, he gave her the once-over and retained his dark, brooding look. Susan sighed loudly. The sound filled the room. She rose, shrugging into her winter coat. The silence was as bleak and gray as the autumn weather outside.

"Can't we at least be friends again?" she said finally.

"I don't know," Steve remarked quietly. "I don't seem as able to categorize my emotions as neatly as you can."

"Meaning what?"

"Meaning as long as I don't get in the way of your ambition, you want me in your life. The minute our responsibilities or goals collide, I get a fast good-bye from you. That's not how I see myself living the rest of my life, Susan."

"You're being unfair."

"Just honest."

A silence darker than the first engulfed them. Susan picked up her handbag. She focused on the shiny metal clasp. "I won't be leaving for several weeks." Her head lifted. Tears shimmered in her eyes, but she refused to let them fall. "We could make good use of that time, see one another again. It's up to you." Her heart was hammering so loudly she thought she could hear it.

"To what purpose?"

"I don't know. You tell me. Think about it." Susan turned and left the office. She had made the first step toward reconciliation. The rest was up to him. Still, the future with Steve had never looked bleaker.

Fortunately, her session with the judge went much better. He was very understanding of her situation, and swiftly made arrangements for Susan to complete her community-service debt.

Somewhat relieved, Susan returned to her apartment and put in a few more hours on her book. Then, needing a break, she went over to her parents' home to talk to her mother. Emma, upon hearing how threatened Steve still felt, tried to comfort Susan. "Honey, give it time. I know Steve. He'll come around."

"We haven't got time." Susan scowled at nothing in particular and leaned against the kitchen sink.

Emma removed several carrots from the vegetable bin and grated them into a salad. "You could make time if you wanted."

"What do you mean by that?" Susan asked.

Emma sent her daughter a level look. "You could put off even looking for another job until you had your relationship straightened out."

"Mother, really, how old-fashioned." Susan retorted sourly. "No, if Steve wants me, he has to take me career and all."

"Meaning, I suppose, you're still not ready to compromise?" Emma queried lightly.

Susan had come home for comforting and sympathy, not a lecture on sacrifice. Patiently, she tried to make her mother understand. "My ambition is as much a part of me as my eye color. I couldn't get rid of it if I tried."

"And besides that, you don't want to," Emma guessed.

"You're a working woman. You ought to know how I feel!"

"I do know how important your work is. And I'm not suggesting you give it up forever. I'm just suggesting you take some time off to discover how you really feel about Steve, about marriage, about commitment. If you were ever really serious about making this on-again, off-again relationship with Steve work—"

"That's just it," Susan interrupted hotly. "We haven't got a relationship. Not anymore." She turned around anxiously. Her hands gripped the countertop edge until the knuckles were white. She felt numb from head to toe, numb and distressed. And hurt by Steve's continued coldness toward her.

Emma couldn't suppress a tiny half smile. "It seems to me I heard that same declaration the last time you broke up." With single-minded determination, she rinsed vegetables in the sink.

"I was right then." Susan began to set the kitchen table for three.

Emma stopped what she was doing. Grabbing her daughter by the arm, she gently propelled Susan into a chair and sat down beside her. "Were you? Susan, let me tell you something. I love working as much as anyone else. And I fought hard to get where I am. But my satisfaction in my job is nothing compared to the sense of accomplishment I have in regard to my marriage. I love your father dearly, and I'm not ashamed to say he is the most important factor in my life." The depth of her conviction underscored every word.

Susan blinked back the tears she felt welling up in the corners of her eyes. "You and Daddy are different." Susan focused defiantly on the wall clock. She hated these heart-to-heart lectures from her mother. They always made her feel she was in the wrong.

"If you believe that, you really are fooling yourself. Relationships are hard. Loving is hard. Being a success at a job in comparison is a snap. Because a job only demands eight or ten or sixteen hours a day. Marriage, as it should be, is a lifetime commitment. The demands a love like that make upon one are endless. But there's nothing that can compare to the richness of a relationship after thirty or forty years of loving one another. Nothing, Susan. No job, no matter how fulfilling, is going to compare to the satisfaction you'll feel when you realize you've built a lasting marriage or a love that will endure.'' Her voice softened. ''Because that love is something no one can take away from you, not ever. That love will warm you and comfort you and give you the strength to endure when you need it most. And to live life without that love would be the greatest tragedy of all.''

''Don't you think I want to have all that?'' Susan felt the tears slipping down her cheeks unbidden. Furious with herself for showing the weakness, she dabbed at them blindly with the back of her hand.

''Not enough to forsake your pride and to do whatever it takes to make peace with Steve or hammer out some workable understanding.'' Emma captured Susan's hands. ''I'm not saying all this to hurt you. I do want you to try to work things out with Steve. Because job offers will come and go. But finding a man like him is rare. Hold on to that love, Susan. Nurture it and give it time to grow. If you don't, you may regret it for the rest of your life.''

Susan wished she could differ with Emma. She couldn't. She was already beginning to regret losing Steve in her heart.

''IF YOU ASK ME, this fight between you and Susan is really stupid,'' Eric informed his older brother over dinner that same evening. "You wouldn't stay mad at me this long."

Steve cut into a piece of pan-fried chicken that was tough and dry. Normally a competent chef, he couldn't seem to cook a hamburger without burning it anymore. And his unusual ineptitude in the kitchen was even worse after the run-in he'd had with Susan earlier that day. He still couldn't believe he'd treated her that badly. Yet once she was in his office, his emotions had just taken over. It was going to be harder to let her go than he'd thought. But, letting her leave without even trying to convince her to stay seemed like the cowardly path to take. Steve had never been cowardly.

Abruptly, Steve realized Eric was looking at him strangely. With effort, Steve concentrated on winning the argument with his brother. "I'm mad at Susan for very good reasons, none of which are any of your business, pal."

"Susan couldn't have done anything that bad," Eric pressed, hoping for information.

Steve was silent.

"You wouldn't stay mad at me this long," Eric tried again.

"You haven't gotten yourself arrested—yet," Steve replied.

Eric pushed soggy, overdone peas around on his plate. He was too polite and experienced in living with his sometimes-volatile older brother to mention that the peas were inedible. "You've read her articles in the *Bugle*. You know why she got involved in that demonstration," Eric pointed out calmly. "If you ask me, you ought to be proud of her." He finally ate a soggy

French fry and washed it down with a big gulp of water.

Steve scowled, pushing his nearly untouched plate away from him. Something must be wrong with him! His brother's simplistic view of the world was beginning to make sense—too much sense! "I didn't ask you."

"Then maybe you should," Eric followed suit, pushing his own plate back, too.

"Eric, enough!" Steve held up both palms in self-defense.

Eric debated ten seconds, then said, "Why don't you go see her?"

Steve shook his head and rested both forearms on the table. "She probably wouldn't let me in the door." *Especially after the way I acted this morning,* he thought.

"How do you know if you don't try? Besides, she's not going to be around much longer, anyway. The least you can do is make peace. She did help you with your campaign." Eric hastily began gathering up his silverware, napkin and glass.

"I suppose you're right about that. The brochures she put together have gotten a very favorable response." Steve got up from the table abruptly and carried his own plate into the kitchen.

"Don't worry about the dishes. I'll do them." Eric stopped him from opening the dishwasher.

Steve shot his younger brother a puzzled look. "Am I hearing right?"

"Think of it as an insurance policy." Eric grinned, ducking his brother's teasing shadow punch. He held up both hands and backed away, still laughing. "I figure the sooner you call a truce with Susan, the sooner you'll be in a good mood.''

Steve shook his head and went up to shave. His kid brother had a point. They had to resolve their situation one way or another. Maybe it was time he let the past go and started concentrating on the future—their future—again.

SUSAN DECLINED EMMA'S INVITATION to stay for dinner and drove home without even the radio for company. She told herself she was a fool to listen to her mother as she let herself into the house. Emma was getting even more sentimental lately. Yet she couldn't deny she did miss the warm moments her mother and father seemed to share. She had lived a life with Steve and without. With him was undoubtedly better, even when fraught with tension. The possibility of a future for them seemed sketchy at best. She did know she didn't want it to end between them as unhappily as it had before. She wanted Steve for a friend. And if not that, she at least wanted peace between them. But first she needed to finish her book. She only had three pages left to type and then proofread. The cover letter and title page were already done. Once the manuscript was safely in New York, she could really relax and concentrate again on making things right with Steve.

The next half hour passed swiftly. Exhilarated to be finished and feeling a vast amount of relief, Susan was just getting up from her typewriter when the doorbell rang. She was tired and aching all over. It has been a long haul.

She opened the door to the chill of an autumn night and achingly familiar smoky-blue eyes. She had to swallow hard to get rid of the sudden clot of emotion in her throat. "Steve." Her surprise at seeing him was revealed by her delighted whisper. Remembering how they had parted, her body stiffened, becoming more wary.

Steve could have kicked himself for doing anything to have caused that hurt, vulnerable look. Suddenly, he wanted to do nothing but erase the hurt they'd caused one another. Recently, and far in the past. Sensing she would reject any physical overtures from him, he kept his distance. His hands clenched around the gift he'd brought for her. "Mind if I come in?" His voice was low and fraught with tension. He held a bouquet of white daisies in his hand.

In answer, she held open the door. He wore a dark blue plaid shirt, jeans and a worn leather jacket. The brisk scent of his after-shave soothed her. Never had she been more glad to see him. "Thank you." She accepted the bouquet of flowers he pressed into her hands. "They're charming."

"They're my way of saying I'm sorry." His eyes held hers for an impossibly long moment. "I've let the election get to me." That, plus the knowledge she would be leaving him again soon, Steve amended silently.

They had both made so many mistakes. She didn't want to punish him any more than she wanted him to continue to punish her for actions that could not now be changed. She dipped her head in acknowledgment. Abruptly, she felt deeply ashamed of herself for all the havoc she had caused in his life during the past month. "I could have been more considerate." She could have put Steve's needs above those of everyone else.

"But that wouldn't have changed your actions," he said softly.

"No, probably not," she conceded. Surprisingly, though, he seemed to accept that now.

She watched as he removed his jacket. While she hung up his coat, he shut the front door. He stopped when he saw the papers stacked in a box next to her typewriter. "Am I interrupting?" He hadn't called. He hadn't wanted to take the chance of her rejecting him.

"I just finished work on my book." She led him toward the kitchen. "Would you like a cold drink? Maybe a sandwich?" Not having eaten all day, she was tired and hungry.

Steve thought of the loathsome dinner he had tried to cook and hadn't been able to eat. "A sandwich would be nice." He paused, not wanting to put her out. She looked exhausted. "We could go out."

Susan said no. If they went out, they would undoubtedly run into people they both knew. Now that she had Steve with her again, she didn't want to share him with anyone. "I'd rather stay here. Bacon, lettuce and tomato okay with you?"

"Sounds great. Anything I can do?"

She gestured to a stool at the end of the kitchenette. "Keep me company?"

He nodded, watching as she worked, admiring her skill in the kitchen. Was there anything Susan couldn't do well, he wondered. Except maybe maintain a relationship. On that score, he supposed they both deserved a failing grade. Abruptly, he determined they would do better. They had to. Time was running out for both of them. Casually, they caught up on campaign news, her folks and Eric's continuing romance with Wendy.

"Have you given any more thought to accepting the job in Minneapolis?"

She deftly sliced tomato and tore lettuce into sandwich-sized pieces. "Yes, but I still haven't made up my mind."

Steve leaned his shoulders against the wall. One foot was hooked over the rung of the stool. "I don't understand." Though the small wooden stool was almost too dainty for his frame, getting comfortable was the least of his worries.

Susan sighed and met his eyes. Her gaze was level and honest. "I want the job. It's living in Minneapolis that would be the problem. I had hoped to be closer to my folks. At any rate, I'm still looking. I'm going to keep my options open for as long as possible and hope something closer will come my way. I don't have to give the people in Minneapolis an answer until November fifteenth, so I still have a little time to find something closer." She turned back to the bacon frying on the stove.

He watched as she turned the pieces with a long-handled fork. "I'm sorry I was so unsupportive the other day when you told me about the position. I wish I were less selfish, but I can't help feeling ambivalent about your leaving again. I want you here."

"I know." Susan's too-bright smile was the only indicator of the depth of her feelings. "But I don't want to talk about that now. There'll be plenty of time later, when it comes time to make the decision of where to work." She reached up into the cabinet to get down several plates. "In the meantime, there are still many markets left that have yet to get back to me. I've got videotapes of my work out. I'm also going to go down to Atlanta and talk to the cable people there."

"When?" His tone was cautious.

"The interview is set up for the day after election. I'll fly down in the morning and meet with them in the afternoon, then probably fly back that same evening, although I've left my return plane reservations open in case I would need to stay on for additional screening or interviews the next day."

She turned. He was still sitting on the stool. His hands rested loosely on his lap. His eyes were intense on hers. Very quietly, he stood and walked toward her. He stopped just short of her. His arms came up to encircle her shoulders. His cheek rested against her forehead. His voice was low and serious. "I hope you get what you want."

Suddenly, all the feeling she had ever harbored for him was there, making her want to cry and to tell him how much she felt. When she tried, her throat closed up. The only words that came out were a harsh, answering whisper of mutual support. "I hope you get elected." She hugged him tightly. He hugged her back, then released her. She knew then that they were all right. They were on their way back to being friends.

They ate their dinner in a comfortable mixture of silence and laugh-filled chatter. It wasn't until they'd carried their coffee into the living room nearly an hour later that he brought the conversation back around to her immediate plans. He sat down next to her on the sofa. "So what next, now that you've finished your book?" He stretched lazily, and after kicking off his shoes, propped his feet up on the coffee table.

Reminded, Susan scowled. She uncurled her stockinged feet from beneath her and stretched them next to his. "Community service. I made arrangements earlier today to get it all out of the way in the next week and a half."

Steve nodded. "I know." At her inquisitive look, he explained, "I did go over to put in a good word with the judge, after all, but it turned out you'd already talked to him."

Her mouth twisted wryly as she lifted her coffee cup to her lips. "I suppose you've heard, then, that I've been drafted to help organize files and do miscellaneous typing at city hall."

"It's driven the county clerks mad trying to find suitable areas to place everyone. The court is trying to match skills with chores that need to be done."

Susan paused. "So what have you been up to?"

Steve shrugged. His jaw tightened as if he were reluctant to discuss the subject. "I've done some light campaigning, spoken on student safety at several of the county schools."

Did he think her that unresponsive to his needs? Mindful of how thoughtlessly she'd acted on other occasions, Susan tried to show more interest. "Isn't there a 'Meet the Candidates' program at the high school tomorrow night?" Steve had been right when he'd accused her of unconsciously not wanting him to win, she thought dismally. And the reasons were purely selfish.

Steve nodded. "That's another reason I stopped by. I wanted to ask you to go with me."

For a second she couldn't be sure she had really heard right. "After all that's happened?" Susan asked. She wanted him to need her with him. She wanted to be given the chance to demonstrate that her attitude had changed for the better. That she could be a help instead of a liability politically again.

He nodded definitively. His eyes sparkled with the devilry she'd come to expect as he stressed, "*Especially* after all that's happened. I want people to know we're still friends." His hand covered hers. Where they sat together on the sofa, their legs touched in one long warm line. The coziness was welcome, spirit-lifting.

"Is your political image the only reason?" She watched as he traced the veins on the back of her hand with the tip of his finger.

Her hand was clasped tightly between the two of his. "No. I wanted to see you." He shifted to face her. He was still as strong willed and complicated as ever; that hadn't changed. But now he seemed more willing to work on their problems. "I've had a lot of time to think the past couple of weeks, since you've been back. I think I knew all along in my heart we had acted too hastily breaking the engagement when we did. Maybe we were wrong to think we could take up where we left off before so easily." He swallowed and looked away for a moment before turning back to her and continuing. His eyes were dark and thoughtful as he spoke softly. "A lot's changed. We've changed. I think, though, that maybe we can start to make sense of us again—where we go from here, if we go anywhere from here together—if we pick up where we left off before I left for the sheriffs' conference in Charleston and continue to take it one day, one moment at a time."

He was finished scaring her with ultimatums. And he was tired of making promises neither of them could keep. Patience wasn't easy for him, but he was willing to try if she was.

"I'll try." Susan moved into his arms. He kissed her gently, tenderly, as if to seal the bargain.

THAT NIGHT MARKED a turning point in their relationship. In the days that followed, they treated each other as carefully as one would handle cut glass— progressing from lunch to lunch, date to date, with little or no mention of the future. Nor did they sleep together again. Susan was baffled at first by his lack of physical involvement with her, but after a while that, too, became a sort of relief. She confided that to him during her last day of community service. They'd taken a break and were strolling in the park across the street.

"I wanted to give us both time," he said softly.

"You've done that." Her heart was pounding. She wanted him. Surely he must know that.

"Ready for the next step?" His eyes held hers. She read both desire and restraint and a mirrored mood of her own frustration.

"I don't know," she said cautiously. "Tell me what it is."

"A solid block of time together, with no interruptions, no outside pressures, no work. A friend of mine has loaned me the use of his fishing cabin in the mountains. I've got the weekend off. Eric's going to be driving over to Roanoke to spend a few days with Wendy's family. We could drive up on Saturday morning, come back Sunday afternoon."

"The election is just five days away. Are you sure you want to leave Grafton now?" She wanted him to put her first, to love her, but she wasn't about to ask him to give anything up for her sake. Especially valuable time campaigning. She knew full well that demands like that only lead to misery for both of them.

"People have decided who they're going to vote for. Sure, it's a risk, my leaving now. But with you leaving to interview in Atlanta next week, it may be the last chance we have to be together. I'm not asking you to sleep with me again, Susan. I just want to be together."

Did that mean he now thought of her only as a friend? His touch said no, but she couldn't deny the seriousness of his words or the abstinence they had so carefully practiced since their reconciliation.

Yet to give up the chance to be with him one last time was unthinkable. "I'll go with you," she said firmly.

Chapter Thirteen

"I would've assumed it was too cold to fish," Susan remarked as Steve's Blazer neared the cabin. Along with the food, overnight cases and sleeping bags in the rear compartment of the jeep were two rods and a large metal tackle box.

"Now is a great time to fish," Steve informed her enthusiastically. "Moderate temperatures can whet a trout's appetite. The baitfish are still stirring. The rivers are all low now and are flowing pretty slowly so unless we're sadly inept—" he sent her a teasing grin before returning his attention to the road "—we'll have fresh fish for dinner."

Never before had he asked her to accompany him on what she had previously assumed was a sport only he and Eric shared. "You're aware I know nothing about fishing," she cautioned.

He remained convinced of the venture's success. "I'll teach you everything you need to know."

Several miles later, they arrived at the gravel lane leading to the rustic cabin. Built of logs, the one-room cabin was square and much smaller than Susan had anticipated. Steve pulled out gear from the rear of the truck and began loading her down with supplies. No-

ticing the dubious look on her face, he explained dryly,
"Don't worry; it's not quite as rustic as it looks from
the outside. It's got running water from the well, a
wood stove, commode and shower. Electricity from a
generator out back."

"Hey, did I say anything!" she protested.

He grinned, swaggering forward to the door. Very
much in his element, he beamed at her. "It was that
look on your face. Kind of a combination of horror
and dread."

"That obvious?" His mood was contagious despite her efforts to remain cool.

"That obvious. Haven't you ever been camping
before?"

"Not like this." Not with a man. Alone. A man she
wasn't sleeping with but still desired very much.

He paused, anxious to make her happy. "Look, if
you'd rather stay in a hotel, there's a Holiday Inn fifty
miles from here."

"No, this will be fine, really."

Inside the cabin was a surprise. Thick quilts covered the double bed in the center of the room. There
was a table and four mismatched chairs. A braided rug
covered the floor. Though dusty, everything seemed in
fine order. She especially liked the wide stone fire-
place.

Steve dumped the rest of the gear in the center of the
floor and glanced at his watch. "It's almost noon. We
better get started if we want to get in any fishing today." He tossed her a pair of battered hip boots that
belonged to Eric. A rumpled fishing jacket with lots
of convenient little pockets followed. "Put those on,"
he said. "I'll bring in some wood and get the fire ready

to light. We'll want it nice and warm in here when we come back.''

Susan disappeared into the bathroom, vastly preferring the conventional facilities to the woods. When she emerged several minutes later, Steve was all ready to go. On top of his head was a hat practically decorated with lures. He offered her one just like it. ''Eric's hat?'' Susan asked.

Steve nodded. He eyed her appreciatively and whistled long and low. ''Looks better on you.''

They walked the distance to the stream in companionable silence, Susan following Steve's easy lead over the semirough terrain. Wild brambles crowded the woods. Leaves crunched beneath their feet. Their breath punctuated the frosty air. Susan estimated it to be about forty degrees and was glad for the warmth of her flannel shirt, sweater and jeans beneath the fishing gear. Steve bypassed several large pools of water, heading upstream. ''What's wrong with these places?'' Susan asked as he took her hand, helping her over a slippery spot.

''The uppermost pool—in a string of flat pools— harbors the more aggressive trout.'' He stopped minutes later at the edge of a deep pool rimmed by protruding, upturned roots and tree trunks. The afternoon's damp chill assaulted Susan's face as she watched him methodically bait his hook with a minnow and effortlessly cast into the pool. Looking reluctant to leave his own line, he nonetheless propped his own rod on a stick and turned to help Susan with hers, instructing her in the rudiments of baiting a hook and using a rod. ''Will I catch something if I just leave my line in there?'' Susan asked.

"Maybe," Steve said. "Trout don't like to chase very far for their dinners this time of year." He picked up his own fishing rod and reeled at a pace to maintain a tight line. When Susan uncapped the hot thermos of coffee they'd brought along, he set his rod down to drink some with her. They munched on sandwiches without speaking. Susan was almost afraid to talk above a whisper for fear she'd scare some fish away. But she didn't mind the silence. It was nice just being with Steve. When their lunch was finished and she was ready to continue fishing, Steve said, sotto voce, "You can jog the lure along the bottom, bouncing it in short hops so it flutters down again like an injured, struggling minnow." He was enjoying his role as instructor. "And sometimes it pays to leave a spoon motionless in a hole for a spell, then bring it to life haltingly." He reeled sporadically to show her what he meant. "Want to try it?"

Susan nodded. As she reeled in her own line, Steve stepped behind her. Arms over hers, his body close to hers, he talked her through the proper way to cast. Over and over they practiced, the warmth of his arms coaxing her steadily into the rhythm of the movement. When he stepped back to let her continue on her own, Susan's line slapped the water roughly. "Aim your cast higher," Steve coaxed softly. Susan did. "Perfect." He smiled, and that expression alone was enough to light up her whole day.

Susan smiled back. "I might be a pro yet, hmm, sheriff?"

He couldn't suppress a very wry grin. "Keep dreaming." His tone was teasing.

Susan's drive to achieve took over. She became determined not only to become competent in his sport but to catch the first trout of the day. Steve was equally intent. Moments passed. Susan drifted, daydreaming lazily as she watched the cloudy sky overhead. Steve's low ''whoa'' was the first indication something was up. Susan gasped in excitement as a strike tugged at his fishing rod. In a flash, Steve snatched up his pole. A scant moment later, a brown trout wriggled above the river. It plunked back down into the water, running against the lightly set drag. Susan watched, glowing, as Steve reeled it in. By the time he lifted out the glistening twelve-inch fish, she was ready with the long-handled net. ''Way to go, Markham!'' she congratulated.

''A beauty,'' Steve agreed. He was smiling from ear to ear. ''But I bet we can catch some even bigger.''

Again, he was right. Hours later, they walked toward the cabin with a string of four fish, the largest measuring twenty inches. The quiet, darkening afternoon added to the intimacy. ''Glad you came?'' Steve asked.

''Very.''

Their glances held. Steve unlocked and opened the cabin door. He knelt to light a fire while Susan climbed out of her hip boots and removed the fishing jacket and hat. ''I'll clean these outside if you'll cook them.''

''Deal.'' Susan had read up on the necessary facts about cooking trout before they'd left, just in case. A small cookbook had been packed into her suitcase. She hadn't wanted anything, even a lack of culinary expertise, to spoil their day.

By the time Steve had come into the cabin with his catch, it was dark. Susan had the stove heating. ''Smells good,'' Steve remarked, hanging up his own coat on a wall hook by the door. He paused at the kitchen sink to wash up. "What is it?"

"Corn bread, cooked in a skillet." Susan lifted the lid to show him. "I've got a bottle of wine on ice. I thought we'd have home fries and some slaw I brought from home." As Steve was paying for the gas, she'd brought all their food.

He grinned. "What had you planned if we'd come up empty-handed?"

"More of the same ham we had for lunch." She affected an exaggerated grimace. "I thought bringing a steak would have shown an appalling lack of faith."

"My kind of woman."

Though the remark was casual, she glowed. "You look very lovely, Susan." In his absence, she had also showered briskly and changed into clean corduroy trousers and a bulky turtleneck sweater in a shade of blue that flattered her turquoise eyes.

"Thanks."

"Have I got time to hit the shower, too?" he asked. Suddenly the air in the cabin was tense. His sleeping bag and air mattress sat in the corner. Though he hadn't touched or kissed her once during the duration of the afternoon, Susan hadn't forgotten how it felt to have him standing behind her, instructing her in the ways of handling a fishing reel. Or how it felt to have him stretched out beside her after making love.

"As much time as you like. The fish ought to soak a bit in salt water, anyway."

While he showered, she stretched before the fire, loving the coziness of the room, the warmth of the glowing fire and the smell of the freshly baked corn bread. The whole day had seemed timeless—no distractions, no television or radio. Susan hadn't known it was possible to achieve such serenity, unaided by anything but herself and the man she shared time with. She hadn't expected the time alone together to be in itself so fulfilling. And yet it was. Maybe her mother had been right, after all, Susan mused. Maybe making her relationship with Steve right again was all that mattered.

The bathroom door opened. Steve emerged, clad in fresh jeans and a masculine red-and-blue plaid flannel shirt. His hair was slightly damp. He smelled of after-shave and soap, and all her senses came to life. Susan had been lounging on the pillows. She sat up. Eyes dark with desire, he looked her up and down, longing etched in his face. "How about that wine?" he asked casually. Too casually.

Susan nodded.

Cooking dinner was just as extraodinarily intimate as fishing had been. Together they breaded the fillets in beaten egg and cornmeal; then, when the potatoes were almost browned, they fried the fillets in butter and cooking oil. They ate before the fire, sitting cross-legged on the floor. Contentedly, Susan licked the last bit of lemony fish from her fingers. "That was heavenly," she said, sighing.

Steve grinned, equally relaxed and content. "Wasn't it?" he murmured, never taking his eyes from her face. "Nothing beats a day or two outdoors." And time alone with Susan.

He glanced at his watch again. The hours were already going by too quickly. "I'll wash, and you dry?"

"Fine." Susan had thought the activity would ease her awareness of Steve. She couldn't have been more wrong. Every time he dipped his hands elbow deep into the sudsy water, she thought of how strong and gentle his arms could be. When he finally rolled his sleeves back down and she hung up her dishcloth, she was aching to be held, touched, kissed. Susan had never been especially shy, and now she coaxed herself to show her feelings to Steve. It was time he knew how she felt.

She turned toward him as she reached over to snap off the overhead light. Darkness descended over the room. Slowly, her arms encircled his shoulders. His lips were soon grazing her hair, then trailing ever so lightly down her face, pausing above her lips. "I told myself we weren't going to do this," he whispered. "I told myself we wouldn't complicate our relationship with passion. But I can't help it, Susan. I want you. I think I'll always want you."

"I want you," Susan whispered. "I love you."

For a second he said nothing, and then their lips were together again. It was warm and sweet and blissfully perfect. She clung to him, loving his strength. He moved against her, alerting her to the intensity of his desire, and a low moan escaped her lips. "It's been so long since you've held me," she murmured.

"Much too long," Steve agreed softly. Her answering kiss was the encouragement he needed. His lips parted hers, first stealing inside to taste, to savor, to taste again of the tantalizingly sweet flavor. His hands swept over her breasts, her hips; he molded her torso to his. At the first suggestion of his desire, her knees went weak. Feeling the surrender, the need that was every bit as great as his own, he laced a forearm beneath her knees and swept her up against his chest. Wordlessly, he carried her to the edge of the bed, then eased her to the floor. Susan swayed against him, watching as his hands moved to the edge of her sweater. Slowly, he helped her out of it, then bent to kiss the upper curves of her breast before releasing the catch to her bra. He continued until she stood naked before him, bathed only in the glow of the fire, the night silent and dark around them.

Her hands trembled as she worked free the buttons on his shirt, the zipper of his jeans. Her remaining doubts fled as he eased her down gently into the sheets. The shock of moving flesh against flesh inflamed her further. She responded to the feathery touch of his hands, learning anew the hard contours of his frame. ''There's nowhere else in the world I'd rather be,'' he whispered.

To Susan, it felt as if they were the only people in the world. She delighted in the soft words he whispered in her ear, words of passion and need, the tender-rough kisses, caresses that laid bare the needs and desires of her soul. Even as he touched her, she ached to be touched again and again. Petal-soft fingertips drifted over the satin of her thighs, found her center, touched and evaded until a ragged moan sounded low in her throat.

His lips moved to her breasts, and the tightness of her nipples seduced him as much as her subtle moan. She could feel his arousal throbbing against her thigh and hear the catch to his breath. Impatiently, she reached for him, wanting their joining to be complete. But he wanted no quick moment of pleasure. When they bonded this time, neither of them would ever forget; neither of them would be left untouched. His mouth trailed fire in an erotic path down her body, tasting, touching, evoking shiver after shiver. ''We have hours,'' he whispered softly, ''hours.'' His mouth found hers again; it seemed forever before they ended the evocative kiss. Odd, she thought weakly, how he could coax from her such passion even as he demanded... She clasped him to her fiercely, resisting sharply when he took her wrists capitulating breathlessly as he claimed her, body and soul.

With long, slow strokes he brought her to the pinnacle of rapture. Contentment surrounded them both. For long moments there was nothing in the room but the sound of their breathing. "Don't leave me," she whispered, nestling against him. She felt that if he did, she wouldn't be able to bear it. "Sleep with me."

"Yes." Too soon, he was reaching for her again, showing her what they had yet to discover, driving her to the very limits of her endurance. And when she thought nothing more was possible, he made love to her again. And then again.

SUSAN AWOKE, wrapped in his arms, their bodies blissfully tangled. Steve stirred in his sleep as she nudged closer. She rested her face on the plane of his chest, content, thinking, *This is all I'll ever need or want*. The thought, sleepy but honest, surprised her. She sat up, half in wonder, half in irritation at herself. She was doing it again, rushing in, expecting everything, when in reality the dividends were bound to be much less. He hadn't even said he loved her, at least not in words. In ways of passion he couldn't have been more explicit, more giving. No, whether he said the words or not, she knew he still cared about her deeply. He needed her on the same inner level she now seemed to need him. But it didn't solve their problems. It didn't make what they wanted the same.

"Susan." A large hand eased over her shoulder, startling her from her thoughts. She was pulled back down beside him. Effortlessly, he flipped his body over hers. "Come back here. I need you."

His arousal was potent against her body. Now was not the time to talk, she thought. Now was the time to feel, to enjoy. "Tell me you love me again," he murmured, tracing the shell of her ear with his mouth. A shiver passed through her, then another, as he kissed his way down the nape of her neck, beneath her chin, to the other ear. If he'd been privy to all the secrets in the universe, he wouldn't have known how to please her any better.

"I love you." She arched up against him, her worries forgotten in the heat and the passion of the moment.

"And I love you," he whispered into the silk of her neck, holding her tightly. Her trust in him was total, and yet she was vulnerable, so giving. He might have been the stronger, but she was equally as capable of making him lose his control. It was a power and a glory that belonged only to her. He moved above her again, propping his weight on his forearms, placed on either side of her head. He marveled at the fact they had made it so far together, that she was his. "For the moment, that will have to be enough, won't it?" His husky tenor revealed the depth of his feelings.

She saw then that he needed answers as quickly and positively as she needed a solution to their dilemma. But answers like that would take time. All she could give him now was her heart and her soul. "Yes," she whispered, easing her arms back around his neck and pulling his mouth back down to hers. They stared at one another luminously, dazed by what had passed and the ardor driving them still. She initiated a soul-searing kiss. "Yes, yes, yes." Together they proceeded to discover again all the many erotic ways there were to love and be loved in return.

Chapter Fourteen

Susan glanced back at the cabin as Steve slammed the tailgate of his jeep shut. "Why so sad?" He tapped her lightly beneath the chin. Although he was trying hard to remain cheerful, there was a definite subdued aura to his mood, as well.

A mist of tears burned Susan's eyes. She refused to let them fall. She forced a tremulous smile. "Fishing was fun. I hate to leave." She didn't want their time together to be over.

"You can always go again." He was watching her steadily. His voice was calm and practical.

"With you?" Silly as it was, she wanted him to ask her to marry him again. She wanted more than this day-by-day arrangement they'd gotten themselves into. An overnight with Steve, a few hours here or there, simply wasn't enough for her, she realized with a start. It never would be.

"Sure. If you're back here, we'll go together." He sounded as uncertain about their future as she was. Susan nodded and stepped past him. What more could she expect from him? Wasn't this what she had yearned for, the freedom to come and go as she pleased and as her work required with absolutely no pressure at all from him?

Steve lingered a moment, watching her climb into the jeep. He could have kicked himself for hurting her that way, but in reality he had no choice. He couldn't pretend their lives were as intertwined as both of them would have liked.

The truth was, he was feeling the same depression. Though earlier they'd intended to spend the early part of the day fishing again, they'd been unable to get out of bed. He hadn't wanted to let her rise, even at noon. It was going to be tough, watching her walk out of his life again. But he knew now more than ever he had no right to keep her captive in rural West Virginia. Susan would end up hating him for it eventually, and he couldn't bear the prospect of her animosity. He'd rather see her leave him. He'd rather make it a clean break, as painful as that was bound to be.

Susan climbed into the front. As he climbed in behind the wheel, she struggled with the recalcitrant safety belt, finally pulling it free of the retracting mode. It was an effort not to help her with her seat belt. These days he found himself wanting to do everything for her and with her. He wondered if she had any idea how much. Teaching her how to use a fishing rod and reel had been sheer heaven. He grinned, recalling her softness, her warmth. Susan's questioning voice jerked him from his thoughts. "Why is it you never took me fishing before?" He'd gone from time to time with Eric or Frank Winter.

Steve shrugged, starting the engine. "I didn't figure you'd enjoy it." Rubbing his hands together and adjusting the dials on the heater, he gave the Blazer a few minutes to warm up.

She put from her mind the tender way his hands felt on her skin and smiled self-effacingly. "I never asked to go because I didn't think you'd want me along. You know, macho man and all that."

He thrust the jeep into gear. "I guess we didn't know as much about each other as we thought."

We still don't, Susan thought. "I'm glad you brought me up here."

"So am I." He seemed about to say more but abruptly cut himself off.

They drove back to Grafton in silence. It was late when they got in, and Steve dropped her off without so much as a good-bye kiss. Susan was grateful that they hadn't rekindled anything sexual. Emotionally, she felt bereft. How was it possible they could have been together for so short a time and leave her aching for his kiss? Was this misery she felt a part of love or just a signal something was terribly wrong, that they were hopelessly mismatched, after all? She knew what she felt, that it was the first premise, but she didn't know what Steve would say. And it was that total loss about what was going on inside his head that disturbed her most of all. She wanted to know what he was thinking. As the woman who loved him, she ought to know instinctively what he was thinking and feeling. But in many ways she was more mystified than before. She felt he was holding so much back from her.

The next day was a busy one. Steve didn't call. But then, she hadn't really expected to hear from him. The day before the election, she knew he would be busy, but his silence hurt. Trying not to think about it, Susan prepared for her job interview in Atlanta. She wrote another short article for Patsy on the aftermath of the mining incident.

When Tuesday morning dawned, Grafton was inundated by light winter rain. Susan voted early. Inside the private voter's box, she stared at the ballot indecisively. Unfortunately for her conscience, her reaction wasn't as much of a surprise as it should have been. For a long selfish second, she was tempted not to vote for Steve. But a vote for Robert Wakefield was pointless and she couldn't do it.

That evening, she attended the party for Steve being held at her parents' home. As she helped her mother in the kitchen, Emma brought the conversation around to the subjects Susan did not want to discuss. "So, are you all ready for your interview in Atlanta tomorrow?" Emma asked, mixing another bowl of punch.

Susan watched her mother pour ginger ale and fruit juice into the glass bowl. "All set, Mom." Susan plunked ice cubes out of trays and then refilled the trays with water.

"Then why the worried look? Steve is going to win. I'm sure of it. Everyone I talked to this morning at the polls voted for him, and our telephone survey was also positive."

Susan dried her hands on a dish towel. "I know. I'm sure he'll win. Maybe that is part of the problem. I wish he weren't so determined to stay here."

"That must have been some weekend you had together in the mountains," Emma observed.

Susan nodded. She lifted her face to her mother's, watching the older woman through a film of tears. "I still love him, Mom."

"Does he know that?" Emma asked gently.

Susan shrugged and turned away. But the third degree from her mother wasn't what she wanted. "Of course." Susan gripped the countertop, staring out the kitchen window at the dark, rainy night. The gloom outdoors matched her mood perfectly. Feeling more composed, she turned back to her mother. "But there's no answer. His life is here. Mine is wherever the best opportunity is."

Emma's lips pursed together disapprovingly as she arranged cookies on a tray. "So neither of you has talked about the future despite all the time you've spent together these past weeks."

Susan's voice was low, tinged with a self-conscious attempt at humor. "We've avoided the subject like the plague."

"What would you do if Steve asked you to marry him again?" Emma shot her daughter a straightforward look. Susan thought of the wedding dress hanging in the closet, the dreams and hopes she'd had for the two of them.

Determined to keep sanity a part of their conversation, Susan explained, "He hasn't asked me, Mother." If he had...

"You still haven't answered my question."

"I'd...probably consider it." Susan shrugged. Her heart raced at just the possibility. But beyond the romanticism was the reality that it would never work.

"Consider, Susan?" her mother echoed exasperatedly.

Susan threw up her hands and gave up the charade. "All right, I'd think seriously about it." Susan took a deep breath. "The weekend convinced me that maybe loving someone is more important than personal gain, in terms of a career or anything else. But that may not make any difference now.''

Emma seemed to feel very differently. Her tone remained cautious. ''Have you told Steve how you felt?''

''No. I didn't want him to feel obligated to ask me to marry him just because we were once engaged.''

Emma chuckled. ''Honey, I know Steve Markham. He's not about to ask anyone to marry him out of obligation, even you. But in this instance I agree with you. I don't think you should wait around asking for him to marry you any more than I think you should take a job halfway across the country again when it's clear you're in love with a man who lives right here.''

''What should I do?''

''I'll tell you what not to do. Don't lay all this on Steve. If you want to stay in Grafton, stay. Don't force Steve to play the heavy again. It's not fair to either of you.''

''What if...'' Susan swallowed hard. ''What if I stay here, Mom, and sacrifice everything and it doesn't turn out?''

''Then it doesn't. But at least you'll have known you tried your hardest to make the relationship work. You won't have to spend the rest of your life worrying about what might have been.''

''You're right. Thanks, Mom.'' Susan moved forward to give her mother a hug.

''Don't mention it.''

Susan moved back into the crowded living room in search of Steve. Eric saw her and waved. He made his way through the throngs of volunteers, Wendy at his side. Both of them looked radiant. ''Hi, Susan. Looking for Steve?'' Eric asked.

"You guessed it!" Susan grinned.

"He headed out back with your dad a few minutes ago. They were going to look at a problem with the gutters at the back of the house."

"In the dark and the rain?"

Eric shrugged. He coughed lightly to conceal his laughter. "You know Steve. He feels there's no time like the present to fix any problem. Your dad says the best time to see the leak is when the water is in the gutter. Besides, they had a flashlight."

"Good for them." Susan's tone was acerbic.

"Good for whom?" Patsy and Frank Winter joined the group. Patsy thanked Susan for the article she had just turned in for publication in the next morning's paper. "There's plenty of room for you at the *Bugle*, either part- or full-time. I wish you'd think about it."

"I have. But newspaper reporting is old hat to me. It's something I could do in my sleep."

"Always looking for challenges, hmm, Susan?" Patsy grinned. A veteran employer and member of the work force, Patsy understood Susan's view only too well. "Good luck in your interview in Atlanta tomorrow. And remember, if you change your mind and decide to stay, my offer is always open."

Susan thanked her and went in search of Steve. Her dad was long gone. The candidate was sitting safely out of the rain, on the glider on the back porch, his legs spread out lazily, his elbows propped on the floral cushion behind him. His head was tipped up in the direction of the night sky. Rain poured down softly overhead, drumming lightly on the porch roof and dripping down the eaves. "Want company?" she asked softly.

Steve glanced up. Pleasure shined briefly on his face. He scooted across the glider and patted the place beside him. "Have a seat."

Susan joined him. The night was cold, and she shivered. He slid his arm around her shoulders but made no attempt to pull her near. "Nervous about your job interview tomorrow?" His question was casual, bearing the same tone he would have used with an acquaintance.

Strangely, Susan wasn't nervous. She shrugged. "I'll either get a position there or I won't." Suddenly, it didn't matter so much anymore. Her feelings of failure had inexplicably eased. The work of time, she wondered, or just being subject to Steve's consoling presence, his faith in her abilities?

He watched her carefully.

She spoke, searching his face with the same intense scrutiny. "Patsy offered me a full-time job at the paper."

"You're not going to take it, are you?" He seemed alarmed that she might even consider it.

"I don't know." She paused, studying him, then teased, "Afraid I'll cause chaos again with my choice of articles?"

He laughed at that. It was a rich, wonderful sound, filling up the emptiness of the night. He responded seriously. "It wouldn't challenge you, Susan. You'd be miserable within a month."

"You're right." She contemplated her parents' backyard grimly. What was she going to do about her future?

He reached over and took her hand. "Go to Atlanta tomorrow. See what you can work out. If they offer you a job and the terms are good, I think you really ought to take it. If not, there is always the job in Minneapolis. You could say yes to that." He meant every word.

"What about us?" Susan turned to face him, bewildered by his attitude.

"We'll see each other as often as you can get back to Grafton. Or I can get to wherever you are." He spoke easily.

"That didn't work before," she pointed out.

He nodded, as if grudgingly accepting the blame for that. He turned her palm over and pressed it between the warmth of his hands. "I wasn't reasonable about the situation then. I know now what it takes for you to be happy. The night at the mines, I watched you talking on camera. You were so good, and I was so proud of you despite my anger. I realized then that there truly was no holding you back. I wouldn't respect myself if I tried."

The words she'd been waiting a lifetime to hear suddenly went flat. "Career success isn't all I want out of life, Steve." She knew from her experience in Lansing just how empty a life with work only could be.

His voice was delicate and strong. "No, Susan, but it's a very large part of what you do want. I realize that now. I'm willing to accept what time you have to offer me and let it go at that." The unselfish gesture was affecting him more than she knew. He wanted to take advantage of her vulnerability and whisk her off somewhere to elope with him before she changed her mind again, his own election be damned. But he couldn't do that, not without hurting her more in the long run. And he'd hurt her enough as it was.

"What about marriage?" She wanted to scream, *What about me? What about us?*

"Maybe, someday. Again, I'm not about to make any promises I can't keep. If elected, I've got two more years of service to complete here."

A torrent of grief swept through her. It was happening all over again, much as it had before. Their dual responsibilities were keeping them apart.

"And then?" She could feel her throat closing up. Somehow she kept the disappointed quaver from her voice.

"I don't know. Eric will be off to college by then. I guess I'll see." He couldn't tolerate any more of being alone with her right now. His control was hanging by a tenuous thread. He glanced at his watch. It was nearly midnight. "Shouldn't you be going home to get some sleep?" he asked softly. He wouldn't be responsible for her botching up an interview.

"I wanted to stay to hear the election results." She wanted to somehow cut past the barriers still keeping them apart and work everything out.

"You know how slow they are in counting ballots here. We probably won't have a definitive reply until three or four. Go home and get some sleep. I promise I'll phone you when we know for sure, before you leave for the airport."

Susan stood reluctantly. She stood on tiptoe to give him a kiss. The embrace remained as chaste as the light peck she gave him. "I want you to win, Steve," she said honestly.

He nodded perfunctorily. "I want you to win tomorrow, too."

Chapter Fifteen

"How'd the interview in Atlanta go?" Emma Trent asked her daughter two days later. It was four-thirty in the afternoon, and Susan was exhausted.

"Much better than I expected. They offered me a job!"

Susan's father beamed proudly. Emma looked torn, both happy and worried for her daughter. "Tell us all about it."

Susan sank into an easy chair and kicked off her shoes. She reached forward to rub her aching insteps. On impulse she decided to draw out the suspense. It wasn't often she had such an interested, captive audience. "Well, to begin with, that Mountain East Airlines commuter flight out of Clarksburg is murder. They didn't even serve peanuts!"

"Susan!" Her father pleaded with exaggerated impatience. "Have a heart!"

She grinned. "I thought that would get you," she teased lightly. More soberly, she continued, "The cable station wants me to do seven sixty-second information spots a week as part of their midday news lineup. The salary is roughly half of what the station in Minneapolis was offering. But for the first time my work hours would be very flexible, at least at first. And there's ample opportunity for me to move up there, once I've proved myself.''

''Are you going to take it?'' Emma asked, leaning forward in her chair.

Susan nodded. ''I start next month.'' Emma's disappointment was apparent. ''But,'' Susan continued softly, ''I'm going to continue living here in Grafton. Because of the brief amount of airtime, I can commute. I'll set up an office here to do my paperwork and wade through research and go into Atlanta three or four days a week to film.''

''Is there going to be opportunity for you to grow creatively?'' Clayton asked.

''They didn't promise me anything, Dad. I liked that. I figure it's up to me to make my own opportunities.'' She glanced at her mother. ''In my personal life, as well. Where's Steve? I tried calling him from Atlanta as well as the airport here, but there was no answer at his home. His office said he'd taken a few days off.'' She was mystified that he hadn't said anything about it to her after they'd last talked.

''He went fishing in the mountains again. Apparently he's staying at that same cabin the two of you bunked at.''

Susan's heart began to race. Carefully, she asked, ''Is Eric with him?''

''No, he's staying with us for a few days. Steve didn't want him to miss school. But he needed some time to himself.''

''Was he happy about winning the election?'' He had seemed very subdued on the telephone when they'd spoken before she left for Atlanta.

"Not as elated as I would've expected," Emma observed.

Clayton added, "I think he was pleased to realize the people wanted him again as head of their county law enforcement."

Susan smiled. She was very happy for Steve. He deserved his success. "What about Robert Wakefield? How'd he take the loss?"

Clayton laughed. "His speech was just sour grapes. Rumor has it he intends to stay with his uncle's glass factory in Clarksburg."

They talked a few more minutes about other election results; then Susan stood. She gave in to the urge to run off quickly, knowing her parents would understand. "I want to tell Steve my news in person, so I'm going to drive up and see him."

"Good for you!" her mother stated emphatically.

Her dad grinned. "You've got my best wishes, too, hon."

Susan smiled. "Thanks."

It was after dark when Susan reached the cabin. The travel-related exhaustion she'd felt before had faded with her anticipation of seeing Steve again. She hadn't dreamed it possible to miss him so much, but she had. She could only hope he felt the same about being away from her. Still, as soon as she pulled her car to a halt in front of the rustic cabin, she felt a moment's anxiety.

He opened the door and stepped out. The light from the cabin formed a yellow rectangle behind him, illuminating the yard. "Susan?" His voice was hoarse. He stood as if in shock, not moving.

She emerged from the car. All the emotion she'd been suppressing for days suddenly welled up in her throat. "I thought you might want company."

Before she could take two steps forward, he had walked across the wet grass and snatched her up in his arms. She reveled in his fierce hug. It was the most delicious warmth and pressure. His body was solid against hers. When he finally drew back, he was grinning from ear to ear. "Let's get you into the cabin."

As they walked, he had to keep reminding himself he had promised not to pressure her. The words "marry me" were uppermost on his mind. Hand clasping her firmly above the elbow, he guided her inside toward the fire roaring in the grate. Something simmered on the old wood stove. Susan looked behind him, her eyes shimmering with excitement and love. The job interview in Atlanta must have gone very well, Steve surmised. A little of the joy he felt faded, to be replaced by anxiety.

"No fish?" Susan asked, taking off her coat and tossing down her handbag. She wore sophisticated clothing, similar to the suit she'd had on the day she returned to Grafton.

"Didn't catch a thing today," Steve admitted. He shoved his hands in his pockets. His smile was lopsided as he commented, "Guess my mind wasn't on the sport."

Her eyes softened, becoming luminous. "What were you thinking about?"

"You. How'd it go?" He decided he would personally go after the management in Atlanta if they hadn't treated her right, or ever failed to do so in the future.

Susan kicked off her shoes and walked over to curl up on the double bed. "I have a job there, doing television spots, but I'm going to be living in Grafton, Steve." The thick quilts were as soft and inviting as she recalled, Susan noted with a soft sigh of satisfaction.

"Do I have anything to do with the decision?" Though he knew it was unwise—dinner would probably burn—he was quickly closing the distance between them.

She tilted her head back to see his face better as he stopped just next to the bed. "You have everything to do with that decision." Moisture shimmered in her eyes, spilled over and ran down her cheeks. Her voice was strong when she spoke. "I want you to marry me, Steve."

For a long second, he was consumed by surprise. Susan didn't move or didn't seem to breathe.

"Is this a proposal?" He talked as if he had a frog in his throat. Suddenly, *he* needed to sit down. He lowered his body. The mattress gave slightly, accepting his weight.

"You bet." She clasped both his hands with both of hers, loving the work-worn feel of his palms. She lifted each hand to her lips, kissing the skin with equal, loving attention. "And I'm not taking no for an answer, either."

He grinned broadly. "You don't have to worry about that. I accept."

"Just like that?"

"I love you. I'll always love you." He took her into his arms. He kept moving until she was lying back among the pillows. Together they uncoiled their legs until they were lying side by side, Steve's body aligned partway with hers.

"I love you, too." Wrapping her arms about his neck, Susan offered her lips up to his for a long, passionate kiss. When they could breathe again, she asked softly, teasingly, "So, sheriff, do you believe in long engagements or short ones the second time around?"

He pretended to contemplate her question for an ominously long moment. "That all depends. What size is the dowry?"

She playfully tapped her fist against her chest, loving the strength and the warmth of his arms holding her close. "Ingrate! There is no dowry. Just me."

"Good enough." He bent his head to hers. He lovingly nuzzled the softness of her mouth. Being with Susan was intimacy defined, he thought. Solemnly, he answered her earlier question. "We can get married anytime you like, though as far as I'm concerned, the sooner the better. We've waited too long as it is."

"I agree." Susan snuggled closer.

"How about before Christmas?"

Susan nodded. "I'm sure my mother and I can get everything ready by then." She laughed abruptly, remembering. "Fortunately, I already have a wedding dress." Thankfully, she hadn't gained any weight, she thought. How embarrassing it would be to have to go out to buy another.

He stroked her neck. "Remind me to thank Emma when we get back for never giving up." Steve paused, his mind speeding past the wedding details to their private celebration.

"When do you start your new job?"

"I won't actually film until after January first, but they'd like me to go down and begin familiarizing myself with their setup and production people in another month."

"Hmm. I'm due back to work shortly, too. I guess that means we'll have to do our honeymooning in advance, then, doesn't it?"

"Steve, I thought you'd never ask..." Susan sighed as she gave herself up to the richness of time and his touch. Moments spun out languorously, like an ever-tightening web of passion and desire, then faded into an eternity of sensual bliss.

"What made you decide to propose?" he asked some time later.

Susan felt she could remain in his arms forever and still never have enough or be able to give him enough. "I didn't want to lose you again. But you were right the night of the election when you said I wouldn't be satisfied simply working at the local paper. I would have gone out of my mind."

"What would have happened if the job in Atlanta hadn't come up?" He was curious, though not threatened. "Would you have taken the job in Minneapolis?"

"No, it was too far away. I would have kept looking until I found something and in the meantime freelanced articles, perhaps arranged a book tour, even if I had to hire a publicist and underwrite it myself."

"You don't have any regrets about giving up the post in Minneapolis?" he pressed seriously. "It did pay more."

"I made up my mind to stay here before I went to Atlanta," Susan confided quietly. "I want to share my life with you. I realize now that my commitment to you has to take precedence over everything else, including my work."

"Do you think you'll be able to switch priorities that easily?" He laced his hands through her hair, loving the way it felt, sifting like silk through his fingertips.

"No. It won't be easy, but the past few months have been a start and you know full well how stubborn I can be once I make up my mind to do something." Softly, she continued. "It's taken time and soul-searching, but I realize my expectations toward marriage and you were very unrealistic. I've given up my idea of the fantasy husband who would follow me around, give endlessly to meet my needs and yet never make any demands of his own on me."

Steve nodded understandingly. "I've given up the idea of having a wife who would be satisfied just being my spouse and making everything else in her life—including her career—secondary. And strangely enough, it was Eric who made me see that." He rolled over so that she was beneath him.

"How so?" Susan asked curiously.

"His relationship with Wendy looked like it was doomed from the start, right?"

Susan nodded, admitting slowly, "That first night I would have bet odds it would never have worked."

"And yet right now they're so happy. They made their love work—by sheer force of will." Steve's mouth twisted ruefully. "I figured if Eric could do it, so could I. So could we." He held her to him for a long moment. Drawing apart slowly, he said, "We're on the right path now, Susan, but we still have a lot to work out."

Susan nodded, loving his tender regard for her. "I know now that demands will be made on us. We'll have to work out solutions together, stick by one another for richer, for poorer, in sickness and in health, in career crises and reelection campaigns." The marriage vows that before had been a mystery now made sense.

He bent and kissed her again, affirming, "With love and the strength of our commitment to one another, anything is possible, Susan. Anything."

She nodded solemnly, her love binding her to him and him to her, for eternity. Softly, she proposed, "Let's reach for the stars."

Harlequin American Romance

COMING NEXT MONTH

#137 CONVICTIONS by Beverly Sommers

Madelyn never expected to find Eddie on her doorstep. They had been pen pals for three years, but he had never told her, in his letters, that he was being released from prison. Nor, she realized, what crime he had committed. Now that he was out, what did he want from her?

#138 THE EDGE OF FOREVER by Barbara Bretton

Meg Lindstrom feared success. Years ago she put down her camera after her sister's heroic death. Now at the bequest of her mentor, Meg has one last job to do. Only Meg never planned on working with novelist Joe Alessio—a man who will challenge both her talent and her heart.

#139 JACKPOT by Judith Arnold

Money. A river of it poured from the slot machine and pooled at Lucia's feet. Cameras clicked, a crowd gathered and Lucia felt ill. She didn't want the money; it brought out people's greed. Like the stranger beside her. Was he taking charge of her and her newfound wealth—or was he taking *advantage* of them?

#140 EVER SINCE EVE by Pamela Browning

Blacklisted by the mill owners, Eve had exhausted all conventional options. What Derek and Kelly Lang offered was not precisely a job but more a service they needed rendered. All Eve had to do was sign the papers that would bind her to the Langs for at least nine months—the time it would take to carry their child to term.

WORLDWIDE LIBRARY IS YOUR TICKET TO ROMANCE, ADVENTURE AND EXCITEMENT

Experience it all in these big, bold Bestsellers— Yours exclusively from WORLDWIDE LIBRARY WHILE QUANTITIES LAST

To receive these Bestsellers, complete the order form, detach and send together with your check or money order (include 75¢ postage and handling), payable to WORLDWIDE LIBRARY, to:

In the U.S.
WORLDWIDE LIBRARY
P.O. Box 1397
Buffalo, NY
14240-1397

In Canada
WORLDWIDE LIBRARY
P.O. Box 2800, 5170 Yonge Street
Postal Station A, Willowdale, Ontario
M2N 6J3

Quant.	Title	Price
_____	**WILD CONCERTO**, Anne Mather	$2.95
_____	**A VIOLATION**, Charlotte Lamb	$3.50
_____	**SECRETS**, Sheila Holland	$3.50
_____	**SWEET MEMORIES**, LaVyrle Spencer	$3.50
_____	**FLORA**, Anne Weale	$3.50
_____	**SUMMER'S AWAKENING**, Anne Weale	$3.50
_____	**FINGER PRINTS**, Barbara Delinsky	$3.50
	DREAMWEAVER,	
_____	Felicia Gallant/Rebecca Flanders	$3.50
_____	**EYE OF THE STORM**, Maura Seger	$3.50
	HIDDEN IN THE FLAME, Anne Mather	$3.50
	ECHO OF THUNDER, Maura Seger	$3.95
_____	**DREAM OF DARKNESS**, Jocelyn Haley	$3.95

YOUR ORDER TOTAL	$_____	
New York residents add appropriate sales tax	$_____	
Postage and Handling	$___.75	
I enclose	$_____	

NAME _____

ADDRESS _____ APT.# _____

CITY _____

STATE/PROV. _____ ZIP/POSTAL CODE _____

WW3R

Just what the woman on the go needs!

BOOKMATE

The perfect "mate" for all Harlequin paperbacks!

Holds paperbacks open for hands-free reading!

- TRAVELING
- VACATIONING
- AT WORK • IN BED
- COOKING • EATING
- STUDYING

Perfect size for all standard paperbacks, this wonderful invention makes reading a pure pleasure! Ingenious design holds paperback books OPEN and FLAT so even wind can't ruffle pages—leaves your hands free to do other things. Reinforced, wipe-clean vinyl-covered holder flexes to let you turn pages without undoing the strap...supports paperbacks so well, they have the strength of hardcovers!

Snaps closed for easy carrying.

Available now. Send your name, address, and zip or postal code, along with a check or money order for just $4.99 + .75° for postage & handling (for a total of $5.74) payable to Harlequin Reader Service to:

Harlequin Reader Service

In the U.S.
2504 West Southern Avenue
Tempe, AZ 85282

In Canada
P.O. Box 2800, Postal Station A
5170 Yonge Street,
Willowdale, Ont. M2N 6J3

MATE-1R